sarah mine

Jenna Howard

ISBN: 978-1-7751134-3-0

Let down by everyone in her life, a desperate and broken young woman overdosed while her newborn son slept. Five years later, Sarah James is trying to forgive herself and reclaim the pieces of herself that she lost. Sober from pills and alcohol, Sarah has one last destructive addiction to purge from her heart. Hill Deveraux.

Everyone knew whose bed he climbed out of. He's the one man she was never able to walk away from, earning her a reputation in town.

Disinherited and disenchanted, photojournalist Hill Deveraux has returned to his hometown and Sarah James. A quick tumble in her bed and things usually look better for him. However, the Sarah he's come back to has changed from the girl he walked away from.

There are secrets in her sad eyes and she's doing everything in her power to push him away.

Hill is going to have to man up and figure out what she means to him, because every time she tells him to go he's unable to stay away.

When he learns Sarah's secrets nothing will ever be the same.

For Sarah & Hill…it's been a long time coming but I finally got it right.

chapter one

SARAH

SOMEONE WAS ON my porch. Even from the edge of my lawn I saw the hiking boots on the railing. The front porch light was on, a beacon guiding me home after my shift at the bar ended. Although I couldn't see who it was, I knew. Only one person would be on my front porch at this hour. I fisted my hand then shook it out in a feeble attempt to stop the slight tremor at the realization. Anyone but him.

Anyone.

I'd take a serial killer…or a religious fanatic asking me if I'd found God in my sinful life…or a creeper from the bar…or anyone but him. Because my heart was doing stupid, crazy things like beating a little faster in anticipation of seeing him while fluttering with nerves because I so didn't want to see him again. Why me? Out of everyone in Pierce Point, why me? I pressed a hand to my stomach.

I didn't want this. I didn't need this. Though many would say I deserved this.

William Hilton Deveraux was back.

For now.

As I approached the steps, one boot lowered with a solid thud followed by the second one. My heart pounded hard at each thump. My palms grew damp as he stood.

I was not ready to see him. I was not ready to see if I was finally strong enough to evict him from my life. Closing my eyes, I wished him away. It didn't matter how many times I told myself over the years that I was stronger. He was here and the truth was mortifying.

I wasn't sure I was stronger. Not when it came to Hill.

"Hello, Sarah."

Four years. Four years since I'd heard his voice. Four years since I'd seen him. Four years since I'd touched him. Four years. *Be strong. Be strong. Be strong.*

I opened my eyes and stared at the man before me. Yep. He was really there.

His hair was shaggier than I remembered, and lighter from the sun. There weren't a lot of barbers where he took his camera. I wondered where his lens had taken him this time. I'd be lying if I said I hadn't followed his career in the photos he sold to books and magazines.

His eyes were different.

They were graver than they had been in his teens. The

things he had seen through his lens had left their mark on him. The silver color was somber now. The poor little rich boy was long gone but that wicked bad boy glint had matured into something that made my chest hurt. I didn't want him hurting.

I dug out my keys, then unlocked the door and led the way inside. There was the rasp of him lifting up his duffle bag though I didn't watch. If I made eye contact, all those promises of no more Hill Deveraux would shatter apart.

I turned and he was there. An imposing figure of every teenage dream I dared to dream. He reached up to tuck a strand of hair behind my ear and my flinch didn't go unnoticed. We both froze. His gaze moved over my face, a little frown appearing as he tried to puzzle something out.

His finger slid down my cheek and my heart stuttered as unwanted memories began to stir. He'd show up, I'd let him in, we'd have sex, then I'd wake and he'd be gone. Every time. All the time. Constantly. From the time he left Pierce Point the first time, until the time he left the last time. And me? I'd bury it all beneath booze and pills. Anything to forget that no one wanted me for more than their own means.

No more, I promised myself. "Shower is down the hall on the right." Easing away from him, I tossed my keys onto the coffee table. "Couch. Night."

"Couch?"

It was three in the morning. I was tired and dealing with Hill was beyond my abilities at the moment. Tomorrow I would face the reality that he was back. "Couch."

"Sarah." My eyes closed at how he said my name. *Be strong, be strong, be strong.*

Because I could not go back. I could never go back to being that girl Hill wanted. The drunk. The addict. The invisible piece of ass. I couldn't be her ever again.

"The couch or the door, Hill." I stopped and looked at him over my shoulder. He frowned at the couch as if he could incinerate it with his eyes, thereby getting himself into my bed. So much had changed over four years. I had grown in ways he would never imagine, nor notice unless he looked. And Hill never looked. He was selfish, the poor little rich boy.

He was sexy.

He was my weakness and that meant he had to sleep on the couch.

"Good night."

Loneliness flashed through his eyes. I would not weaken.

Once inside my bedroom, I shut the door while lecturing myself. Four years had taught me a lot. I had cleaned up. All addictions eradicated. Including Hill Deveraux.

I wiggled out of my bartender's uniform, thankful to no longer have Brandi's written over my left breast in hot pink thread. My pants fell to the floor and I froze when I heard the shower.

"Pretend he's not here. He's not here." I changed into my pajamas, then crawled into bed.

Hill was back.

I should have gotten him sheets was my last thought before I sank into the welcome oblivion of sleep.

HILL

I didn't know this house. As I washed away the grime of travel, I admitted I wasn't too sure of Sarah either. She said no. To me. She never said no. Bracing my hands on the tiles, I stared at the drain as I tried to process that I was going to be sleeping on the couch. I didn't want to sleep. I didn't want to dream. I wanted to forget.

I wanted to forget myself in Sarah's body. Jax had once said that Sarah was the magnetic north for my dick. Maybe. But being with Sarah was effortless. I didn't have to drag out some charm. I didn't have to seduce my way into the pair of panties of a girl whose name was already forgotten. Being with Sarah was easy. And I desperately needed easy right now.

Once I felt more human, I dried off, then, naked, walked down the hallway to the living room.

The couch. My mind was dulled from being awake for too many hours. I lay down and listened to the hum of the fridge and the utter solitude of Sarah's house. Fuck, it was quiet. My skin itched as if I was still covered in sand and grit. The room felt too small. This house was creeping me out without me knowing why. I didn't want to be on the couch.

I didn't want to be in Pierce Point any more than I wanted to be on this fucking couch that was too narrow, too short, and too empty.

"Fuck this."

Rolling to my feet, I walked down the hallway. I may not know the house, but I knew the owner pretty damn well. The odds of her kicking me out of her bed were pretty slim. This was *Sarah*.

After my eyes adjusted, I saw the bed and the bump under the covers. I went to the other side of the bed and slipped in next to her. The sheets were cool against my skin while the feminine body was warm.

This I knew. She smelled right. She felt right. Caressing down her back, I stared at her. *Sarah*. It would be so easy to nudge her legs open and slip inside her. It would be so easy to lose myself in her. *Find* myself in her. A soft, sleepy sigh escaped her and I lowered my cheek to her shoulder.

There was no more silence with the soft sounds of her deep breathing. And, I admitted as I pressed my nose into her hair, the loneliness eased enough for me to sleep.

SARAH

Somebody was in my bed and he was naked. His breaths were slow and warm against my ear. The arm stretched along my side was heavy and the hand spread on my thigh was familiar. A smart woman would get out of bed with a naked Hill occupying half of it. Even knowing better, I still ran my finger over the back of his hand. A tiny touch couldn't hurt me right?

His skin was warm, proof that he was real and I wasn't hallucinating. Tears burned in my eyes and my chest felt tight. He was here. I wasn't surprised that he had made his way into my bed. I should get out of bed and kick his naked ass out of my house.

Instead, each of my fingers slid along his. Silly Sarah. This was not smart.

Holding my breath, I eased over so I could look at him. With him asleep, this was the safest time to do so.

He was so gorgeous he made my heart hurt. At the very beginning I wondered why he was in my bed. Then I came to the realization that he was in my bed because I never said no to him.

Even with his face relaxed in sleep, there were lines at his eyes and two bracketing his mouth. My finger hovered above a silvery scar on his right cheekbone. When had he gotten that? How?

The face was familiar, but the changes weren't. He was only twenty-six, two years older than me, but he seemed much older. As if the pictures he took aged him.

He inhaled a deep breath and his hand slid down to cover my ass. Dark gold lashes lifted. William Hilton Deveraux. Heaven and hell all rolled up into one tasty package. Dark grey eyes and dark blonde hair, he was sin. He was my greatest downfall. Forget the drugs and alcohol, this was my addiction.

I tried my damnedest to ignore the insistent press of his erection. *I need to get out of bed*, I thought a little desperately as his hand slid to my hip and along my waist before he guided me onto my back. He sprawled half on me, a heavy weight I didn't want to remember so vividly.

"Sarah." He said my name quietly, as if speaking loudly would spook me. Maybe it would. He lowered his head and kissed me.

Resist! I needed to treat him like the addiction he was. Quit. Maybe go to rehab over him. Attend H-A, Hill Anonymous, meetings. Find a sponsor. Anything because this…

This was a bad idea.

His lips parted over mine, nudging me to join in the seductive play of his mouth. I couldn't do this. Not anymore. The routine hadn't changed over the years. We'd fuck. He'd leave. I'd fall apart. I couldn't do that again. I could not be that girl again, not even for Hill.

I cupped his face and felt the sharp press of his cheekbones, his face leaner than I remembered. Seeing his photographs tore at my insides. I couldn't imagine living them. He had, though, and what he showed on film had left impressions on his body and spirit, because his eyes were still tired and haunted.

"I can't," I whispered, astonishing both of us. Could I do this? Because, no lie, he felt so good lying on top of me. The heat of his body was intoxicating as it soaked through my pajamas and he was hard right where I wanted him. No, I didn't want him. I couldn't want him. This is how it started and I couldn't go back. I couldn't. Going back scared me. Terrified me.

"You can, baby."

I shook my head as I gazed up at him, his fingers lightly gliding up and down the curve of my waist. Did he see? Did he even notice I had changed? That I wasn't mind-numbingly drunk or high or any of that? Did he even realize that I wasn't the girl he had left four years ago?

He lowered his head to kiss me and I knew the answer. No, he didn't see. Because that wasn't what we were about. We were the fuck then the leave. Over and over and over again. Turning my head, I looked at the clock hoping it would tell me what to do.

"Sarah," he whispered in my ear as his hand made its bold move from my waist to between my legs. A jolt of heat made me jerk as if the cotton of my bottoms didn't exist, and he found all the right places. His fingers rested lightly over me, the middle one rubbing in slow strokes.

Holy. God. My toes curled as my eyes closed. That one little touch caused massive cracks in my resolution because it felt so good. It was hard to deny what he did to me. My body knew him, craved him. The thin fabric that separated his finger from me grew damp.

His name escaped on a broken sigh. Betrayed by my own lust. Lips rested against my neck, his breath hot and moist on my skin as he teased and tormented me. And himself, if the heavy weight of his erection resting against the inside of my thigh was any indication. Every brush of his lips made my skin burn, and his hand moving between my legs ignited me.

"Look at me."

Swallowing, I opened my eyes as his weight shifted. The pillow under my head dipped a little. He braced his right arm above my head, his left one ceasing its torture.

Shifting, I met his gaze. His fingers slowly caressed up the front of my pajama bottoms then slipped under the elastic waistband. My stomach jumped at the heat of his fingers; the calluses added an extra something to the caress. The minute he hit that damp, aching spot, I cried out, arching into him.

His gaze shifted over my face before returning to my eyes. Arousal burned in the silver depths as he watched me writhe. A little smile, the tiny flare of victory as he pushed a finger into me. Even as I cried out, arching at the sensation, reality swept through me as I stared into eyes that knew he had me. His easy fuck was a few strokes away. I wondered if he even liked me. If he even saw me as a person. He made my heart hurt in the worst possible ways.

Oh God, I couldn't do this again. I gripped his wrist and the teasing touches came to a sudden halt. He frowned down at me, frustration churning in his eyes until that glint of satisfaction was gone.

"Why? Damn it, why?"

"I can't, Hill."

"Why?"

We both knew I could. The evidence was between my thighs, my body slick and ready for him. His hand shifted, damp fingers resting on my stomach then sliding to my hip. He rolled us both so I lay on him. This was almost as bad as him on top. There was just too much temptation in Hill. "Because I really want to," I admitted before easing away from him.

I sat on the side of the bed, his heated "Fuck" echoing around the bedroom. Anger, frustration, confusion. I heard it all in his voice. It took all my tattered will power to stand and leave him in my bed, because I was feeling those too. He was naked; he was aroused. He was Hill.

And yet, I was walking away.

Because I couldn't go back. I couldn't go back to that fragile, broken shell of a human being that had been with him four years ago. I had barely survived being that girl the first time.

The second time would probably kill me.

chapter two

HILL

I FOUND A mug. I found the coffee. I found the woman sitting on the railing of her back deck while she drew. Damn, but she was pretty with her messy brown hair and the pajamas that left little to the imagination. If my camera were in my hands, I'd fill a roll of film of her. Right now.

I leaned against the railing, looking at the yard and not the sketchbook. Sometimes she'd show me what she drew but mostly she didn't. Her choice. I respected that. Not everyone saw all the photos I took. My stomach gave a little twist. "How long have you lived here?" I needed her to talk to stop my thoughts from forming. That's why I was here. To forget all my shit.

The black fine tipped marker halted its faint scratching movement on the page. "Almost three years."

I sipped the coffee as I looked through the open sliding door. The house wasn't big. A little bungalow that was older than me with two bedrooms. Did she own or was she renting? I was curious. And a little envious. My current place of residence was a hotel. If one were to press for more, I'd admit the majority of my crap was in storage. Storage was easier to maintain when I wasn't home a lot. "Nicer than the apartment."

"A box in an alley was nicer than that place."

The last time I saw her, she lived in a small apartment above the bar her father owned. It had reeked of stale beer and hamburger grease. The party noise below was constant during the night: shouts, music, and laughter. A lot of nights had been passed in that slum. Hours of mindless fucking where I didn't have to be anyone but Hill.

This was nicer but I sure as hell didn't feel like Hill here. I bet if we had been in that old, dumpy apartment we'd both be coming our brains out. Instead, I was drinking tasty coffee with a Sarah I didn't know.

She returned to her sketch and I watched the way her light brown hair fell over her shoulder, forming a partial curtain between her and the world. She looked like the Sarah I once knew. She certainly had the same big, sad brown eyes I remembered. There were still faint freckles on her nose and cheekbones. That was the same sexy mouth. And she sure as hell was still the fragile girl I had last screwed when I was twenty-two.

But she wasn't the Sarah I knew. She wasn't so used up, strung out and gutted by demons I couldn't even imagine.

Everyone knew about Sarah James. Everyone knew what had happened in that James house. Everyone had seen the bruises. Everyone had turned a blind eye to the marks, to the booze, to the drugs. Even me. What an asshole.

Pretty, I thought. She was so damn pretty. Reaching up, I brushed her hair away. She froze like a terrified deer because that's what you did when a hand came at you.

Asshole. Brandon James was an asshole.

So was I.

She looked cautiously at me and I wished I knew what went on in her head. If this were four years ago, we'd still be in her bed. It wasn't, though. I traced the rather delicate line of her jaw. I shifted so I stood between her knees and set her sketchbook aside.

"I can't, Hill." Her voice was soft as she looked at me. She had the biggest, saddest eyes. They gutted me. Slashed through my own crap. They showed every hit she had ever taken, every drink to forget her life. *Sarah.*

"Quiet," I said, studying her face. "I'm taking pictures." And I was. Fast, mental snapshots of Sarah.

This was new. I caressed the cheek that wasn't so gaunt. Her face was fuller and her skin was a soft sun-kissed copper instead of greyish and lifeless. Soft and silky and not so…hollowed out. The eyes were still sad and haunted, but they probably always would be. They had a clarity that hadn't been there the last time I saw her. "Sarah." Her name escaped on a low burst of wonder. "Look at you."

A soft gasp escaped from her and tears filled her eyes, making the color shimmer but they didn't fall. While I was gone, Sarah had kicked the booze and drugs. "Look at you," I repeated softly. Her lashes lifted and she met my gaze. I saw the nervousness in her eyes, felt them in the way she touched my biceps.

"Hill?"

"How long?"

"Three years, one month, and three weeks."

My eyebrows rose. That's…amazing. "That's pretty exact."

"Sobriety is an exact science."

"Good for you. I need a shower, then I want Helena's pancakes." I caressed her mouth. "Want to join me?"

"For pancakes?"

I smiled. "Or the shower. Take your pick." I knew what she'd say.

"Pancakes."

Now I grinned. "Surprise me, Sarah. Say yes to the shower."

"No. Go away." The corners of her mouth twitched though. That was something.

"I give good shower." I winked and surprised myself by leaving her on the railing. Inside her little house, I stopped, pushed off the pants I had dragged on. A startled laugh came from her as I walked naked down the hall and into the bathroom. I had never had to seduce Sarah James before.

And I was going to. Stoned or straight, drunk or sober, then or now…I wanted her. I always wanted her.

SARAH

I fiddled with my pen before I hopped down. Things felt a little wobbly on the inside. That he had noticed I was sober surprised me. Truly I hadn't thought he'd notice or care. I picked up the khaki pants that had seen better days and went into my bedroom. We were going for pancakes.

We *never* went for pancakes. Of course we had never not had sex before either. Tossing his pants on the bed, I contemplated what to wear for this momentous breakfast. Talk would start up. It had probably already begun the minute someone had seen Hill. I knew what they said about me and Hill. Pierce Point was a small town and gossip was its addiction of choice.

Maybe breakfast wasn't smart.

I could almost hear the talk now. "Did you see? Hill Deveraux was at Helena's with that James girl. Oooh, you know what they were up to. Shameful. Carrying on like that. He's a Deveraux! And you know what trash that James girl is."

Funny how I was the one who was trash in my family when my father had beaten me and my sister slept with any man who looked at her. I knew why they called me that and it wasn't the booze, the drugs, or the bad choices I made. The reason was in my shower. One didn't simply sleep with a Deveraux. In Pierce Point you were a Deveraux's wife, a soon-to-be-wife, or his whore.

Was I ready for that to start up again?

"I don't know," I said in the quiet of my room. And that was the problem, wasn't it? What good could possibly come from this? Hadn't the entire point of the past four years been to stop repeating past mistakes? To learn who I was and embrace her, forgive myself for things that had never been my fault, and those that had been?

How was this good for me? I had to treat Hill like I did the alcohol and pills. An allergy that could kill me. An addiction that would make me lose myself again.

I needed to tell him to go.

But deep, deep down I wanted him to stay. And that was the problem, wasn't it? This was Hill and I wanted him. That was my dirty secret. Drunk or sober, then or now…I wanted him. I always wanted him.

Covering my face with my hands, I sighed at the admission. Since I'd become sober, I had learned to be honest with myself.

"Heavy sigh. Deep thoughts?"

I nodded without lowering my hands. *Please don't touch me.* But that's all I wanted him to do. I listened to him cross the floor and my heart thumped fast. Anticipation, nerves, need, fear, lust, and heartache. All were felt when he stopped behind me. So close I could smell the fruity soap and feel the shower's steamy heat radiating off him. His hands on my hips made my eyes close. If I couldn't see him, the problem didn't matter.

Rrrrrright.

"I thought of you in the shower."

That comment dragged out a laugh. "I bet you did."

"Dirty mind, Sarah," he breathed into my ear. Goosebumps spread down my spine at the brush of air. Oh hell. "And no, not those thoughts. Though now…"

I lowered my hands, but couldn't open my eyes. Not yet. That would welcome reality. "So, what were you thinking?"

His fingers slid along the elastic waist of my pajama bottoms. "That you need soap that doesn't make me smell like a bath shop vomited on me."

"Get your own soap. I like my soap." *Step away. Step away!*

"I like your soap too. It smells like you," he whispered in my ear, his hand slipping under the waistband of the shorts. Sneaky Deveraux. Slowly, he ran his hand over my stomach, hip to hip, back and forth. "I had a hard time concentrating as I lathered you all over my body."

My lips parted at his words, the imagery it brought to mind. Hill naked in my shower. Hill wet in my shower.

All he did was lightly touch my stomach and breathe against my ear. Done. I was done.

It was so easy to imagine his hands sliding over his body, slippery bubbles slithering down his skin. Against my ass and through the towel he was hard and it made things shiver awake. A little gasp escaped.

"Oh yes," he continued in that soft, seductive whisper. "You know I did exactly that. I stood in that rather extravagant shower, you on my skin, and lathered you on my dick that was hard as fuck for you. You made me come in your shower." His hand slid down between my legs and I cried out when he found me throbbing and slick from his words. "With you on my body."

He began to caress where I ached, making my body weep for more. He teased the wet entrance with the tip of a finger, making me cry out.

"Had you been in that shower," he continued, the

maddening motion making me wetter and wanting him deeper, "I'd have been able to bury my dick inside you. And you'd be slippery, more than any amount of water and soap could make you, and welcoming. And we'd come. Me inside you. Come, Sarah. Come as I did. By my hand and imagine it's me snug inside you where you're warm and slick, happy to feel me. Come, baby."

I covered the hand between my legs, the fabric damp from what he did to me. I climaxed with a cry.

"Take me, Sarah," he whispered. "Take me where I need to be." His hand slid further between my legs, his touch no longer teasing, but rubbing, his thumb finding that sensitive spot. He kissed the back of my neck as he worked me with hard, insistent strokes that made my hips roll over his fingers. "Bring me home, Sarah," he moaned as he eased his finger in.

I cried out, pressing more against his hand, his finger sliding, the tempo familiar. So familiar. "Hill. Oh God. Please."

It felt so good, him moving inside me, his breaths hot on my neck. "Bring me home, baby."

"Yes," I whispered and he spun us and bent me over the bed in a fast movement. I grabbed the sheets as he pushed the bottoms down and his towel was yanked away.

"Sarah," he moaned. He withdrew his finger. "Oh

God, Sarah."

I nodded and he thrust inside me, his hand, damp from my body, covering mine. After, I would regret. Now, I wanted him. Needed him. Had it always felt this good? I pushed back into him to take more of him. I couldn't remember. I wished I remembered the weekends of sex, the waking up and he was gone, and I'd have another drink to numb the pain. Because, holy God, he felt so good.

The weight of his body against mine, pressing me into the bed as he took me, his moans in my ear as I took him. "This," he whispered. "This. Look at me. God damn you, you look at me."

I turned my head toward him and opened my eyes as much as possible.

"Sarah." He kissed me, continuing his thrusts. His other hand found me and made me scream as I came. His lips curled upwards against mine, then with a moan, he came. I gasped to feel him inside me. My fist relaxed and his fingers slid between mine. "Now."

"What?" My body felt heavy, sated.

"Now it feels like you."

My eyes opened, watching as he lowered his head to the bed. "What?" The word burned inside my chest. Had he just said what I thought he had said? "What did you say?"

I knew what they called me. Hill Deveraux's whore. To hear that from him. Had it been like this before? I wished for one sober memory.

"What?"

"Off. Get off. Get out."

His eyes opened as he eased off. "What? What's wrong? What did I do?"

"It's what I did." I rolled away from him and sat up. Reaching down, I grabbed his towel and wiped us away from between my legs. "I won't go back, Hill. I won't be that girl again." Tears blurred the floor and I could almost taste the sweet rum on my tongue. I hadn't liked alcohol to taste like alcohol. It wasn't a problem if it was in a glass of cola right? Or a milkshake. Or in a glass of ice. I couldn't go back to that girl. I wouldn't live like that again.

"I know. What did I do, Sarah?"

"Not even for you will I go back to being Hill Deveraux's whore. Go. Somewhere else. Anywhere else. Just go. Get out. Leave me alone, Hill."

His eyes had narrowed to slits the color of dark storm clouds. "Back to being who?" He caught my wrist when I went to stand, needing to wash him away. "Back to who? What did you call yourself?"

chapter three

SARAH

HILL HAD A temper. It was a dangerous, volcanic thing. We had gotten into a few arguments over the years. Battles that had ended on the floor with wild, angry sex. Or in the storage room of the bar. In his car. Wherever. But when he fought, he fought dirty. Whether swinging his fist or using his mouth, he fought to draw blood.

"Let me go. You're hurting me."

"No, I'm not, and you know it." He tugged as he stood up. While his fingers were like a manacle around my wrist, there was no pain. It wasn't a bone-crushing, leave-a-bruise grip like my father. "Repeat that again."

"What part? How about the part where I told you to get out!" I screamed the last two words at him.

"How about the part," he shouted right back, "where you called yourself a fucking whore? What the god damn hell is that?" He pointed his finger in my face. "What the fuck, Sarah, is that?"

"Go. Go."

"No way, baby doll. You dropped the "w" word. Where the hell did that come from, Sarah Jane?"

"Everyone, William Hilton. Everyone. Including you." I tried to walk away but he drew me back.

"I'll deal with everyone in a minute. They're not in this damn room. You are *not* a whore. Not mine. Not anyone's. Don't," he said with a little poke of his finger toward me without coming close, "say it again. And I have not, now or ever, called you a whore. I've called you a lot of things but never, *ever* that. What did I say? When we were lying there, what did I say? Tell me. Repeat it."

"That I feel like me. Because I instantly fall on my back for you. Want a fast fuck? Hey, let's go see Sarah." My voice was a mocking bass timbre, imitating his.

Hill's eyes were like a hard storm coming off the bay and slapping the town around. "Shut. Up. Yes, I said it feels likes you. Bank it." He pressed his finger against my mouth, shutting me up. "Come with me." Since he still held my wrist, I had no choice but to follow him into the bathroom.

My sumptuous bathroom. This bathroom hadn't come with the house. When I had bought the place, it had been a simple bathroom. A tub and shower combination, a toilet and a sink. When I finally moved in, the bathroom had become this thing of extravagant splendor. There was a claw foot tub, a separate shower. The walls had been painted a soft yellow that reminded me of spring sunshine, with glass subway tiles the color of summer grass in the shower. Above the tub was a skylight so I could lie back in scented bubbles and stare up at the blue sky.

The renovations hadn't been my idea. The bathroom had been simple and dated when I had seen the photos of the house while in rehab. No, all of this had been a surprise.

Deverauxs were sneaky.

Hill positioned me to face the mirror. "This," he said with a growl in his voice, "is the first thing I saw yesterday." Frowning, I looked at us, trying to figure out his point. He stepped behind me and bent down so our heads were even, and then he pointed at the mirror. "Look at her, Sarah."

My gaze shifted to my reflection.

"Look at her. She's been sitting in the sun, and I think she has a few freckles that I know she didn't have before because she was always pale. Tired. Flattened down. Bruised around the eyes, empty in the eyes." He ran his finger down my cheek and he looked at me, not the mirror. "Who is this girl who isn't hiding in a bottle? Who is this girl with color in her face and who isn't wearing her cheekbones on the outside of her skin? Who is this girl with spirit in her eyes when before they were filled with hopelessness? I don't know this woman. Never seen her before in my life."

I turned to look at him, his grey gaze drinking in every one of my features. "So what? Because we have sex that makes me someone you know?"

"No. It makes me someone I know." He ran his thumb along my mouth. "You aren't the only lost soul in this house."

His words tugged at my heart. Maybe I wasn't the only broken one here. It was a startling thought. All he had said to describe me – that was on his face now. His eyes hid shadows of hopelessness. He was the one who looked tired and beaten down. What had happened to him? Despite all my chaotic emotions about him being back, I didn't want him to be like this. A shadowy reflection of the golden boy he once was.

I rose up on my toes and kissed him, trying to get rid of what was imprinted on his face. "You promised me pancakes, pretty boy."

"So I did." He tugged on my top. "But since you're already half naked, how about you get all naked and we have a late breakfast?"

"I'm not easy, you know."

He smiled.

It was a late breakfast.

HILL

"Nothing's changed."

"Were you expecting flying cars?"

I pointed at her and she smiled. I liked that. That she smiled. I didn't have a lot of memories of her smiling. If any. I'd have to look through my photos, but I was pretty sure there hadn't been a lot of smiles in the pictures I randomly took of her.

Yeah, I didn't know this Sarah at all. But I wanted to.

I wanted to know why she had gotten clean. I wanted to know about the house. I wanted to know everything she had done in the past four years.

It was a strange feeling.

I looked around the Pierce Point Café and saw that not much had changed. The old white and navy blue had been replaced by a pale cream color, so everything didn't look seasick anymore. The walls were pretty much the latest update. These were the same waitresses who had served me pancakes after tying one on as a teenager. I opened the backpack I brought along and eased the lens cap off my camera. Before Sarah could blink, I had the camera up. I caught her image just as her lashes lowered like they always did, but the little rise of her lips still remained and a tiny blush darkened her cheeks. She'd never let me take a picture of her with her eyes looking at me. Even when she had been hammered, she'd hide her eyes from me. It was as annoying now as it had been then.

"Put that down." She reached over and pushed on the camera.

"I still have them, you know."

"Stop it. Put that down or I'm leaving."

I set the camera down on the table because I knew she would leave. I didn't want her to leave. "I love that you don't ask what *them* is." She blushed completely. Resting my elbow on the table, I propped my chin on my hand to gaze at her. "God, you were sexy."

"Shut up. We're in a restaurant. There are kids in here."

"So sexy. Once you got over the shyness, you were so sexy as you lay on your bed. Every glorious naked inch of you caught in my camera. Let's do it again. I'm way better now."

"I am not doing nudies with you."

"Yes, you will."

A frustrated sound came from her and she grabbed the same menu I remembered and held it up. I laughed. Bracing my forearms on the table I leaned over. "You know how I know you will?"

She dipped down the laminated edge and looked at me.

"Your nipples are hard."

"William." She hit me with the menu then folded her arms over her breasts. "You're a lunatic."

"I know. It adds to my allure."

"Good morning, folks. Coffee?"

I sank back and flipped over the white mug with Pierce Point Café written in red script. I lifted my eyebrow, and Sarah looked at the waitress and nodded. I turned her cup over and loved that she picked up her menu again to hide her blush. And her breasts. Sweet.

"I'm having the pancakes. Double stack. Butter on the side and blueberry syrup. Double order of bacon too."

"I'll have the same but a single serving of each."

The order was written down and there was a sudden intake of breath. "William Deveraux! Oh lands, I didn't even notice."

I looked away from Sarah who was adding sugar to her coffee. "Hi, Sally. How are you?"

"Oh I'm fine. A little bit of rheumatism, but you don't care about that. How are you, boy?"

Wrecked and burned out. But one didn't go about saying that. No one gave a damn about my shit. "Doing good."

"Look at you. Still handsome as ever." I half expected her to reach over and ruffle my hair. Sally had always fit my mould of the stereotypical waitress. She had to be in her sixties now but she still dyed her hair a harsh jet black. Too much pink blush, too much orangey-red lipstick. Happy wrinkles on her face, a clichéd style waitress uniform a size too small, and black shoes made for comfort not style. She was friendly, gossipy, and always gave me extra syrup.

Sally glanced at Sarah and did a double take. Sarah lifted her fingers in a wave while she sipped her coffee. There was a tennis match look from her to me. Back and forth. I expected Sally's neck to pop. "Let me get that order in for you. You look half starved."

"And so it begins," Sarah said, setting her cup down. She gave a gasp and pressed a hand to her breasts. "Did you see? William Deveraux is home. Still as handsome as ever."

Grinning, I sat back as Sarah batted her lashes as if they were coated in five layers of mascara, like Sally. Oh, yes, I did like this new Sarah.

"What a troublemaker that boy was. Lands, I remember when he streaked through town upon graduation. I never." She fanned her hand by her neck and I laughed at her little eye roll that said perhaps "Sally" wasn't as scandalized as she said. "And did you see who he was sitting with? He was with that Sarah James girl." Another dramatic gasp. "Oh, there was gossip about those two. Not that I ever believed it. Now I'm not one to gossip but one night they were caught out at the old mill. Naked," she whispered loudly. "Imagine that! Such behavior for a Deveraux." She clucked her tongue. "Such behavior."

Sarah shrugged a shoulder with a little eyebrow lift then sipped her coffee. She was rather brilliant. We had never hooked up at the mill, old or otherwise. But people loved a good scandal and William Hilton Deveraux had been pretty damn good at scandalizing. "Since rumor has us naked at the mill, wanna go flash some skin?"

"Pervert."

"Yes," I said with a stretch. "Yes, I am. And you like that about me."

"Debatable."

"Love it," I mouthed at her as Sally set our plates down in front of us. "Thanks, Sally."

"I heard about your father. Such a pity." Sarah coughed, interrupting Sally and asked for some water.

Just like that my appetite died. I stared at the perfectly golden pancakes and extra crispy bacon. The thought of eating any of it made me want to throw up. A foot nudged the inside of my left leg and I looked at Sarah.

"Fuck them. Eat your pancakes."

"Not hungry."

She tapped my thigh this time and I reached down to squeeze her ankle. I wasn't on speaking terms with my father. If I were lucky I never would be. When I was kicked out, I left town and was gone for a year. My return had earned me the knowledge that I was disinherited, thank God, and there were no more chains holding me to Pierce Point.

I still came back, though. A giant "fuck you" to Big Jack Deveraux and his vision for me.

She lifted a slice of bacon up and held it out to me, waving it beneath my nose to seduce me with the scent of crispy, greasy pig fat. It worked. I caught her wrist, took a bite then reached for my fork. When she went to ease her foot away, I held it in place. I saw the quick look she gave the diners. We were getting looks because word was spreading: Hill Deveraux was back in town. I wondered if they saw a reunion TV show in their head: asshole father and rebellious, disinherited son reunite over deathbed and father lives.

I hoped the fucker died.

chapter
four

SARAH

I LEANED AGAINST a lamppost and watched Hill take a picture of two little girls sharing their ice cream cones with each other. It was cute. Each held a cone while they tasted the other's flavors. He had been silent since the café and I knew it had been the mention of Big Jack. "You knew, didn't you?"

He lowered his camera for a second, then without responding to me, he took another picture of the girls. He turned suddenly and caught me in the crosshairs of his lens. I looked away as the soft snick came. He walked toward me, the shutter whirring as he continued to take pictures. "Stop it. I'll leave."

He lowered his camera, a large piece of expensive-looking equipment that had seen a few years in his backpack. "You have no idea, do you?"

"About?"

He braced his hand above my head and leaned into

me. "Even after everything I said in your bathroom, you weren't listening."

"To what?" He tilted the camera up as he leaned in and kissed me. I barely heard the picture captured.

"Pretty Sarah."

"Bullshit Hill."

He shook his head as he stared at me. "Honest Hill. What time do you work?"

"Seven. I need to start getting ready at six though."

A snort escaped him. "It takes you an hour to put on black jeans and a black shirt? Well, maybe after I strip them off."

I grabbed the front of his t-shirt. "Hey." He sighed and nodded. He knew Big Jack was sick. I left it alone. If he wanted to talk about Big Jack, he would. And since it took a lot of alcohol and a flash of his temper, I figured there'd be no talking about his father. Or even why he was here.

"You know a lot of old stuff is going to come up, right? You're back. He's ill."

"He's dying, Sarah, and it couldn't happen to a better man. Well, maybe your father."

I wondered who had gotten hold of him. It wouldn't have been anyone in town and I couldn't see his mother suddenly tearfully calling her son home. No, the only ones who would've told him anything were his brothers. Jax, I thought as Hill walked down the street, easing his camera back into his bags of tricks. Jax would be the one to call. He'd see it as a courtesy call he should make as the eldest Deveraux brother. Jax was the type of man who, even though he no longer lived in Pierce Point, still seemed to know all that was going on.

I envisioned him having this intricate spy network that told him when his dead-beat dad was sick or I was in the hospital. It was more likely that he had a subscription to the town newspaper, but the spy ring could be possible. This was Jax Deveraux. Anything was possible with him.

For a man who had spent years boasting about his three great sons, Big Jack had done a bang up job of alienating and abandoning all three of them. And I thought my father was bad. At least he loved one of his kids.

We wandered around Pierce Point and I knew it wasn't because Hill felt like reminiscing. Sometimes you just had to try to outrun your demons. He walked and took pictures. And I used to drink. Until I realized demons couldn't be outrun, even after a combination of drugs and alcohol made you face mortality. There were greetings to both of us and a lot of double-takes when they saw who we were with. I wanted to jump on a bench and shout out: "Yes. Hill is back. Yes, we had sex already. Nothing more to see here. Move along."

Interesting, since I was all about keeping things low key when it came to him. Did he notice the whispers? Did he know we were the center of attention? It didn't seem to bother him, but one day I'd wake up and he'd be gone. I was the one who had to live with the fallout.

While Hill darted into the deli, I sat on a bench. What the hell was I doing?

This was me changing things? This was me learning from past mistakes? Because from where I was sitting, I was right back where I had been four years ago. Only this time I was sober enough to know what was happening. What was that saying about insanity? That it was doing the same thing over and over and expecting different results?

What was I going to do when he left? This time there'd be nothing to numb everything. Because it would hurt. It *always* hurt to wake up and find him gone. Not a good-bye, not a note, not a see you later. Just an empty bed and his bag gone.

"Roast beef on sourdough with spicy mustard."

"I can't do this," I said as he dropped the wrapped sandwiches into the side pocket of his pack. He stilled, smart enough to realize I wasn't talking about a sandwich or lunch. Hill sat down, lowering his bag to the bench. He copied my position, resting his elbows on his knees. "I can't be that girl again, Hill."

"We've had this conversation, Sarah."

"I can't be her anymore. I can't be the one they talk about. I can't be the girl you use as a weapon against your dad, this town, or yourself. I have spent almost four years trying to pick up my pieces. I struggle every day to not go back to who I was. And you…you keep breaking me open. I don't know if it's deliberate or not. Does it matter? I know what they say about me here. I know that I could be sober and clean for fifty years and I'll still be 'that Sarah James girl' to everyone. I don't want to be 'that Sarah James girl' to me." I wiped my cheek and stared at my damp fingers. "I think…I think that's how you see me too. If I'm the only one on Team Sarah, okay. But you're not. You're Team Hill. And that team," I shrugged, "sees me as the enemy." I stood. I needed to walk away. Walk away from him, and I guess, walk away from me.

"I do not."

I nodded as I took a step backwards. "Yes, you do. You really do."

"Damn it. This was easier when you were…"

I held up my hand, stopping him from finishing that sentence. "See? Team Hill." Making a fist, I turned and walked away. It was hell. It was like being in rehab and detoxing again.

I'd be okay. I had made it through it then, I could make it through this.

HILL

There were billions of things wrong with Pierce Point. At the moment number one was that the only drinking establishment of any worth was Brandi's. It was rather ironic, or pathetic, that the woman I was drinking over was the woman pouring my drinks.

What drove a sober addict to work as a bartender? Something wrong with that career choice. Lifting my glass, I took a sip of whiskey. When life kicked you in the balls, you asked the alcohol gods for salvation. I hated hard alcohol. I hated the smell; I hated the taste. But I sure enjoyed the efficient way it could get a guy hammered when he was on a mission. Sarah tilted her head to hear over the band that was murdering Bon Jovi. They were terrible. They made my teeth hurt they were so bad.

"Well, isn't this unexpected. William Hilton Deveraux."

Fuck.

I lifted my glass and took a bracing swallow as Brandi James spilled into the seat beside me. Damn, I thought, blinking. Someone had gotten herself a new pair of tits. They were straining the front of her black polo shirt with her name in hot pink swirly, girly letters on the left breast. Subtle. Real subtle. Brandi was as much a brunette as her sister but had gone for the blonde look. It was okay, I supposed, if one cared.

All of the buttons on her top were open, to show off the new boobs, and there was a god damn pink heart tattoo on the impressive swell. It matched the damn apostrophe in Brandi's. That was just sick.

"Hello, Brandi."

She leaned forward. Presenting the cleavage? "How are you, Hill? It's been a while."

"I'm fine." There was something very calculating about Brandi. It had taken a while for me to catch on that she was looking for the richest dick in town. Of course I had been a teenager in high school when I first decided I deserved smokin' hot Brandi James and her incredible vanishing panties. And because I was William Hilton Deveraux, she had decided I was the right game for her ambitions.

She sent me on one long mind fuck. She collected boys in high school, a man harem to do whatever she wanted. I was ashamed to say I had been one of her sheep. And what Brandi had wanted was to utterly destroy her sister, for whatever reason. I had been the weapon of choice.

Yeah, I had bullied Sarah, humiliated her, all to win the girl. Only the girl I wound up with that night hadn't been the one in front of me but the one behind the bar. Talk about a twist of fate.

I hated thinking of that night. The scent of bonfires

and cheap beer had a way of making the small of my back sweat because I'd see her so clearly. Those sad brown eyes got to me, even then, but seeing them filled with fear as the feral dogs that were my friends had circled her was something else entirely.

I wasn't a hero, not now and certainly not then, but even I hadn't been heartless enough to let them drag her off into the night. So I had laid claim to the drunken girl in over her head and had taken her virginity not long after, starting the twisted return and retreat to Sarah's bed.

That had pissed off Brandi. I was supposed to be one of her hard-ons on a shelf; I was supposed to do what she wanted. To have lost the rich kid to her sister? There was a viciousness to Brandi that was hidden in her pretty face. She had been mean to Sarah before we had hooked up; after, it was a cruelty that would've impressed Big Jack.

I glanced at Sarah and figured nothing had changed with the sisters. What the hell was she doing here?

"You look," the tip of Brandi's tongue curled out to touch the little bow of her mouth, "good."

What shit. I looked like hell. "Likewise." What shit. She looked like hell. Well-ridden, put-away-wet hell. That almost made me grin as I finished my drink.

"I've seen your pictures. You're really good."

I was. That was the crux of it all. "Thanks. Which one

is your favorite?"

Her deep red lips parted at the question. Damn but she was a walking, breathing cliché from her fake boobs, to her fake hair, to her fake human appearance. Beneath all the cheap gloss, Brandi was a praying mantis.

Leaning back in the chair, I watched her writhe on the hook she had dangled. If she knew one photograph of mine, I would strip naked and bend her over the table and give her what she wanted. Right there, right then. An eyebrow arched up as I waited. I caught the waitress's eye and held up two fingers then tapped them against the glass I waggled. If I was going to chat with Brandi, I wanted to start doubling up.

"That one on the cover."

Which cover? "Uh-huh," I said, tilting my chair back. Sarah was filling a line of shot glasses with what looked like tequila. She loaded a tray, set a salt shaker and a bowl of lemon wedges in the middle, and it was whisked away to the band. Not helping things, Sarah.

I couldn't help but compare the two sisters, and not just their appearance. Once upon a time, Brandi had been the hottie. She still was if she didn't try so hard to be the girl she had been in high school. She wasn't. She was twenty-six years old, a long way from a bright-eyed teenager. Brandi was the pampered daughter while Sarah had, for whatever reason, become the punching bag. Brandi had been the babe and Sarah the shadow. Somehow in the four years I had been away and Sarah had gotten clean, she had turned into a pretty woman. Not hot like Brandi had been because that wasn't Sarah. But she had come into her own while Brandi had not so much hit the skids, but…stalled out.

My drink was poured. The only reason I knew that was my drink was that Sarah had looked right at me before she poured. *That's right, baby, I'm drinking because of you.*

"You should come by later," Brandi said, "and we can talk about old times."

"Which times were those, Brandi?" The game was tiresome now. It was the same one from adolescence. "The times you teased my dick or led me around by it? Thanks, honey, you made my night," I said to the waitress who set my glass down. "You tell that pretty bartender to keep them coming."

"I forgot, Hill, how much of an asshole you are." Brandi stood up then looked down her nose at me.

"A lot," I said, taking a sip of his glass. I stretched my arms out as I measured how much. "A lot."

She gave a huff and walked away, swaying her ass to show what I was missing out on. I didn't know what a flounce was but I was pretty sure that's what she was doing. I was not missing out on much with that James sister. Well…maybe an STD.

Now that she was gone, I could get on to more important things. Like wondering where the fuck I was going to sleep now that my original plan was screwed to hell and gone.

SARAH

"That, my love, is a sad, miserable sight."

I glanced away from where Hill was drinking. Damon, the other bartender, sidled up beside me. He copied my pose by resting his elbows on the bar.

"What is?" What had Brandi said? Anything about why I had gotten sober? Doubtful. If it wasn't about Brandi, my sister didn't think about it. That my sister had made a play for him wasn't surprising. She *always* did. As if him rejecting her had turned on Brandi's big game hunter vagina button.

Damon looked at me then Hill. His brown eyes were serious, as if he was studying something extremely interesting. "The two of you." He drummed his hands on the table then straightened. "I have not seen this many sneaky-eyed looks in a long time. And I work in a bar. Stop ogling, Sarah, and start dropping panties. That boy is hammered enough to not say no."

I wrinkled my nose at him. "You're an asshole."

He winked.

I wasn't going to drop my panties. That was the problem. An order came in, allowing me to focus on making drinks instead of Hill. When there was a slight break because the band wanted more drinks (as if that would make them better), Hill's table was empty and he was nowhere in sight. I scanned the bar and noticed he wasn't the only blonde not around. Brandi had disappeared too.

When two o'clock rolled around and Damon made the last call announcement, I had never been so relieved to know a night was coming to an end. It typically took us an hour to shut everything down after the last body staggered out after losing their keys to the jar. My father had started having his customers drop their keys in a jar when he had first opened Brandi's, and we'd never lost a car to someone stealing a set of keys. Probably because no one wanted to make Brandon James mad. At noon, they'd all be dropped in the mailbox out front to be picked up. I think the idea had come from my mother. I couldn't see my father giving a damn what anyone did. Not that I was going to ask him or my sister.

Brandi returned to count out the tills while I cleaned up my bar. We were always the first two to arrive and the last two to leave. Brandon James' law. Not even Brandi could ignore it because he took the running of his bar very seriously; even if he didn't want his youngest anywhere near it.

It wasn't because I was an alcoholic, though my father scared me too much to ever dip into the bottles even when I had been drinking. It was because he hated me and wanted me to have nothing to do with his legacy.

Working in a bar probably wasn't the wisest idea for a recovering alcoholic, but I did it for a few reasons. I knew how to do this job and I did it pretty well. And it pissed my father and sister off that a piece of paper legally bound me to this building. Once in a while Brandon would offer a large amount of money to buy me out of my mother's inheritance, resorting to threats of violence when I said no. But the main reason I worked here was because I had made a choice four years ago to not be afraid of my father and sister. He had stopped swinging at me shortly after the overdose and I often wondered if it wasn't because of Jax Deveraux, my unlikely guardian angel.

"So, Hill Deveraux is back," my sister said.

"Yes." I set the boxes filled with empty bottles in a pile beside the bar.

"Oh, that's right. You and he have that thing."

I ignored the snide tone even though it stung. Brandi was one of the frequent users of the phrase "Hill Deveraux's whore." Which was funny since Brandi slept with any guy who caught her attention. "Had," I said, not really believing the word as I went into the office to double-count the trays. Brandi followed. She always did. Our dad came in to collect the cash drawers. No one but him deposited the money. Not even Brandi. I kept my head down as I sprayed the bar with cleaner.

I hated closing down.

I hated the close proximity to Brandi and Dad when all I wanted to do was go home, shower off the stink of temptation and crawl into bed, my feet sore and throbbing. My sister was like a bird of prey just waiting to swoop in. There were many words I'd use to describe Brandi: patient and nice were not two of them. Sure enough, down swooped those deadly talons for a killing strike.

"Sure is a sexy man, and he knows what he's doing."

I paused and returned to scrubbing a sticky ring on the smooth wood. It was hard to argue with either point. He was and he did. He really, really did. Once Big Jack had disinherited him, Hill had fallen off Brandi's radar. He no longer had the financial means to give her what she wanted. He was no longer the golden son of Big Jack but the disgrace who wasn't allowed back into the hallowed halls of Deveraux House. A fall from grace that I knew had hurt, even though his father was an asshole. He had been punished for daring to live his life his way. Pride was something Hill had a lot of.

And guess who had given it a few whacks this afternoon?

"Good night, Sarah. I plan on having a *great* one." To the bone those red colored claws struck. To the bone.

I grabbed my jacket, because even though spring had struck Vancouver Island, the air had a little nip to it that made me thankful for sleeves.

I did not look at the upstairs apartment that had a light burning in what I knew was the bedroom. When I moved out, Brandi had moved in. Brandon had spent a lot of money renovating the small apartment into something bright and airy for his beloved daughter. He had soundproofed it, put in top-of-the-line appliances and plumbing and my sister had rubbed it in.

Still did. My sister loved reminding me that Brandon had a favorite daughter.

If Hill was willing to put his penis anywhere near the Venus fly trap that was my sister as she had been not so subtly implying, well…he was never coming near me with it again. God knows what he'd catch with that toxic vagina. I had a little pride, too.

Everyone had a weakness. Mine wasn't alcohol or drugs; those had been my means of self-destructing. No, I had kicked my weakness out of my life earlier. Hill Deveraux.

I used to think my weakness was being Brandon James' unwanted daughter. Nope. Weakness was what made us vulnerable and Hill Deveraux made me very vulnerable. Being a punching bag for my father and an easy target for Brandi was nothing compared to the emotional chaos of Hill.

It took fifteen minutes to walk home and I was ready for a shower, food, and bed. In that order. I was crossing my lawn when there was a sense of déjà vu. He wasn't on the front deck this time but on the steps. Slowing down, I looked at the man with the slumped shoulders and elbows braced on his knees. The hair that needed a haircut was messy.

He looked up and his eyes shattered me. He looked defeated. As if something inside him had given up. *Hill.* "I had nowhere else to go, Sarah."

Last night the cautious voice in my head had screamed *trap!* Tonight it nudged because I knew what it was like to have nowhere else to go when the bottom was the last stop. I touched his messy hair and he rested his head against my stomach. The weary sigh made me hurt. "Come on, Billy. Up you go."

"I threw up in your neighbor's roses."

"Awesome."

"Someone kept giving me whiskey."

"What a bitch."

He nodded, then sighed again. But this sigh was the sound of someone who had drunk way too much. And did he have it in him to stand up without throwing up on me? I knew this was probably my most unwise decision of the day. Still there was relief and joy that he was here and not with Brandi.

chapter five

HILL

OPENING MY EYES, I wished for death. My head was making it known it was pissed at me; my mouth felt dry and swollen and I wasn't entirely sure all that booze from last night was going to stay down. A glass of water sat on the nightstand table with a little note that said *drink me.* There was a little drawing of me looking like hell. Bitch. I drank some of the lukewarm water and saw two little white pills resting on a piece of paper that told me to *"eat me before you drink all the water."* Goddess. I took the aspirin and finished the water.

With a tired sigh, I lowered my whiskey-soaked head back down then turned to look at the woman in bed with me. She was so pretty, fast asleep. Too bad she was in her pajamas again. She needed to learn the fine art of being naked when we shared the bed. Wasn't that what a good hostess did? Accommodate her houseguest. Even if I was a party crasher.

Holding my breath, I slid out of bed, grabbed my glass, and went to refill it. I had a serious case of too much booze dehydration. I stood in the kitchen and downed two more glasses of water, snagged my camera, used the john, then returned to Sarah. She filled the viewfinder, a curious blend of sweetness, fragility, and sexiness. The shutter clicked loudly in the silence of the room. I braced my arms on the mattress and adjusted the focus so she was slightly blurred. While I had a few digital cameras in my arsenal of goodies, I still preferred the good ol' fashioned film camera. There was something about the weight of it and the soothing sound of the film advancing to the next frame that relaxed me. For work, it was mostly the digital cameras. The world changed fast. Within minutes I could send the photos from my camera to my editors. And I couldn't lie, the bells and whistles on the digital cameras were pretty sweet but to relax, regroup, and center myself…that's where my old camera came in to play.

"Stop it."

"Make me."

She grumbled, and without opening her eyes, turned her face away. Grinning, I reached out and tugged the sheet down and focused on the thin strap of the cami she slept in. The peachy color against her skin, strands of messy dark hair, a hint of her chin. She lifted a hand as if flicking me away. Setting the camera down on the nightstand, I slid in beside her and kissed her shoulder. The faded scent of her fruity soap made me smile as I settled behind her.

I briefly considered seducing her, but after yesterday, I had a feeling if I did, things would skid out of control again. "You often take in drunks?"

"Just the pathetic ones who tip my waitresses really well." A little smile appeared and I lowered my head to her pillow. Her elbow lifted and I took the concession. I slid my hand over to rest on her stomach, loving the soft skin warm from sleep. "Are you okay?"

"Hung over. Too old for that kind of abuse." I liked the way she shifted so we were pressed together. Her artist fingers toyed with mine.

"No. Are *you* okay?"

I studied the back of her head as I thought over the question. The answer was easy. No. Sober Sarah saw too much with those sad brown eyes filled with clarity. Instinct yowled at me to get out of bed and get my ass far away but I couldn't move. Too tired for that. Deep down to my soul, exhaustion was sucking me as dry as last night's truth.

I had nowhere else to go.

"No." That I had answered surprised us both.

We didn't do this. Talk. We fucked. That was the way

with us. I may have spoken a truth to her but I didn't want to talk about the why. The fingers gently sliding back and forth along mine were soothing. "Where was your job this time?"

Yes, Sober Sarah saw way too much. I pressed my lips against her shoulder. "Don't."

The caresses stopped and I felt her entire body grow still. "Why? Because we just fuck?"

"No." Because if I voiced it, that would make it true. Then what would I have? Nothing. Absolutely nothing. I was a guy with a backpack full of cameras and a duffle bag filled with ghosts.

"Right."

My arm tightened when she went to pull away. "Don't," I whispered, my hand fisting on her top to keep her from leaving.

"Why? I'm going to see the photo somewhere, so it's not a secret. Where were you?"

I shook my head.

"Right," she whispered. "Right." She pulled away and I watched her sit up. Her head fell forward and I found myself moving, sitting behind her, my legs against hers.

"No." I banded my arm around her waist when she went to leave. "Sarah." I didn't want to be alone with my thoughts. They were a plague and the cure scared me.

"You think I don't know what you see out there?"

"I think you see more than anyone else does. I'm tired, Sarah. Let's just lie here. Please?" Lowering my head to her shoulder, I shut my eyes. "Please." She nodded once and it was enough. I eased us backwards, drawing her warm body close. A shift of her body and she was facing me.

The hand on my cheek made me close my eyes. Or was it because now she was looking at me and she'd see I was flailing around in my head? Her thumb feathered below my mouth; her index finger was soft beneath my eye.

"Bad boy Hill Deveraux," she whispered, "afraid of little ol' me?" I nodded. Utter truth. Lips lightly brushed over mine. "Why? I'm just the girl you fuck."

My eyes opened while her lashes lowered. This time she was hiding. "No, you're not. I wish you were. Hey, don't get mad and threaten to leave again. We both know you're not going anywhere."

"Asshole."

I smiled as I kissed her. When her mouth parted, something deep inside me roared with primal triumph. Rolling onto my back, I slid my fingers into her hair to hold her in place as our tongues met. I always liked kissing Sarah: from the first kiss to the last kiss. She half lay on me, her body warm and soft. A little sigh escaped her and she slid on me completely as she deepened the kiss, her hand resting on my chest.

I felt her smile and reclaimed her mouth. I traced her spine and fiddled with the hem of her top. I could get her naked. We both knew it. But then it would go to shit again. I wasn't ready for it to go to shit again. A little reprieve. I deserved that much.

Letting her go, I combed my fingers through her hair as she rested her cheek beside her hand. "Can I ask you something?"

Her shoulder twitched in response so I took that as a yes.

"Why is a recovering alcoholic working in a bar?"

She sighed and the soft brush of air caressed my chest, made me think of getting us naked. To hell with the consequences. "I'm good at it."

"No." I tumbled her to her back, pinning her beneath me. I shook my head and she looked down, her fingers caressing my neck. The soft touch made my cock twitch. "No seductive ploys. Tell me why."

Her hand a made a fist and I saw the surprise in her eyes when she looked up. "So you get my secrets but I don't get yours? How is that fair?"

"It's not. I was watching you last night. Why are you working there?"

"Because," she whispered as her eyes filled, "I refuse to be scared anymore. And two things scare me: slipping backwards and…" Her swallow sounded overly loud in the cocoon we had going for us.

"Brandon the Bear?" She nodded. "He still smack you around?" My thumb drew a circle on her cheek, then a line along her nose. She used to sport some hellishly ugly bruises on her sweet face.

"No."

"You feeding me bullshit?" Because, seriously, if he was marking her up, I was going to give the man a come-to-Jesus talk.

"No."

"Little liar. He's a bully and he likes it." A tear slid down her temple and I wiped it away. My head tilted and as I studied her, something began to burrow in my brain and I didn't like it. "He ever come at you, Sarah?" She had been a virgin when we first hooked up but that didn't really mean anything. And there had been the pills and the alcohol. They were a good way to make bad shit disappear.

"No. No."

"Are you lying to me?" I cupped her chin and tilted her head back. "This is it, Sarah. Cards on the table." I had no idea what I'd do if she said that, yes, her dad had molested her. Jesus.

She shook her head as more tears fell. "He didn't. Really. I am not lying to you."

"Then why are you crying, baby?" The tears made me want to find Brandon James and kick his ass. I was man enough to admit I was pretty shitty to Sarah. Why the hell she kept letting me into her bed and her body was beyond me. But what her father had done to her lit a cold rage in my belly.

Sarah cupped my face and lightly pressed her lips against mine. "Because you asked. You never did before."

No, I hadn't. Because I was just as big an asshole as her father. She drew me close again, her mouth a little more insistent against mine as a leg slipped out from beneath me to hook around my hip. "Now you say yes?" I wiped the still falling tears from her face. "No. Let's go get some pancakes."

She gasped. "Hill Deveraux is saying no?"

"Hey, if Sarah James can, so can I." I gave the exposed curve of her ass a slap. "Come on, sweet thing, let's go sober me up first. Then when my head isn't throbbing and moaning…then we'll get back to this yes-no business."

"I have food here."

"Yeah, but you can't make pancakes worth a damn." I kissed her, pushed aside the blankets, and held out my hand.

"How do you know I haven't learned a thing or two?"

Grinning, I leaned over her. "I have no doubt you have, but I've seen what you do to pancake batter and it isn't pretty. At all."

"I hate you."

"And you hate me good, baby. Now put that sexy ass in some jeans and feed me properly." I walked over to my duffle bag and rooted around until I found a reasonably clean shirt and jeans that weren't too bad. "Am I staying? Or are you going to have another kick-me-out-of-your-house moment?"

She rolled onto her stomach and stared at me. I found myself reaching for the camera out of pure habit. "I probably will."

"Well, can I use your washing machine before you do? I have a serious lack of clothes."

She nodded as she climbed off her bed. "It's off the kitchen."

This time I did grab my camera as she drew her top off. I caught the image of her, arms up, fabric at her head and all that smooth back revealed to me. I ignored her demand to put down the camera and she flung the scrap of peach at me. Cami in flight, one breast bared, lashes lowered, and lips smiling. I had it all in one frame. Hips in mid-shimmy as she pushed the shorts down, her cute little ass flashing me while her hair fell forward. Lowering the camera, I watched her draw on a pair of bright pink panties that didn't seem to cover much. Setting the camera down on the bed, I walked around intent on getting to her. I plucked the matching bra from her hands and let it fall to the floor as I took her mouth in a kiss, walking her toward the bed.

"Feeling perkier?"

"Feeling something," I said, sliding the panties down.

"I knew you didn't mean no."

I caressed one leg and leaned over her. She was so damn sensual. It was a part of her like her sad eyes, and her artistic talent. "I'm so easy," I said before lowering my head and kissing her. I swallowed her little, gaspy moan when my fingers reached her warm, slick sex. Her foot slowly ran up my leg, granting me more access.

I knew there had been other men. Hell I'd had other women so who was I to judge. But I wondered if they got this from her, because I couldn't recall her being like this. The booze and the pills had put a barrier between Sarah and the world, and so those rare sober moments in her bed had been exquisite. Raising my head, I watched her arch beneath me while her hands caressed my arms up to my shoulders. "Hill," she moaned as her foot pressed on my ass to get me to move where she wanted me, between her legs and deep inside her.

Damn, I didn't want pancakes. I wanted her. I wanted her writhing beneath me, her body wet and welcoming. She always felt so good. She was the only woman I had been naked in because of that. It didn't matter that I'd gotten a vasectomy at nineteen, a raised middle finger at Big Jack. I never went without condoms except with Sarah.

Her artistic fingers caressed down my arm and over the fingers sliding over her. Ah hell, I thought as I grabbed onto my control with both hands. This was not going to last if she joined in. Her cry made my belly tighten as we both teased her, her entrance weeping for me to fill it. God, she was so pretty. Lashes down, cheeks flushed, mouth parted. I took mental pictures of all of her. Her lush, round breasts with their swollen tips, the way her stomach tightened with each roll of her hips. My brain captured the images to be savored later.

Leaning down, I captured one of her nipples in my mouth and my hand caressed down her leg, leaving her to caress herself as she cried out my name. Little nails from her free hand dug into my ass making me grunt at the sensation. Both her hand and foot urged me forward and it was hard to deny those soft, husky cries, or her hand moving between our bodies. *Sarah.*

I kissed up her arched neck then gazed down at her face. "Come, baby. You're so beautiful when you come." I caressed her cheek. Beneath me, she surged and I felt her body strain against mine as her orgasm sent her over. "So beautiful," I said as I took another mental picture, then slid between her legs and thrust into her. She was tight and wet from the orgasm and I was unable to resist kissing her.

There was nothing like being inside Sarah. Nothing. I could get lost inside her because she made all my shit disappear. Her damp fingers, warm from her body, curled over the back of my neck as she met my thrusts, her mouth just as hungry as mine. We were a couple of fuck-ups, our lives chaotic and messy, but here…here we were perfect. Did she realize that? That when she was like this and I was deep inside her, we were simply Sarah and Hill instead of the two most notorious screw ups in Pierce Point.

"Hill," she whispered against my mouth.

"Sarah," I replied, shifting above her, thrusting harder and faster into her. A tiny smile of approval flicked over her mouth. "Hm, someone wants to be fucked, doesn't she?"

"Stop talking," she said as she lifted her head to kiss me. "And yes."

Reaching down, I grabbed her sweet ass with one hand, adjusted my body, and gave her what she wanted. Ah hell, what I needed too. No thinking, no feeling beyond this. Me taking her and her taking me. She met the hard thrusts of my body as I sought oblivion. Maybe with this orgasm, I thought stupidly, I'd forget all the shit that waited for me beyond her bed.

Still thinking. Not doing this right, William. I took her mouth and her legs wrapped around my hips. There, I thought as her tongue met mine, there. I drank her needy cries and felt her tighten around me. *Sarah.* I braced my arm above her head and watched her as she came. The way her mouth parted as she whispered my name, the way she hid her eyes from me, the way she spilled around my dick. Perfection. *Sarah.* Then my own orgasm grabbed me by the balls and threw me into the fire of her body.

There, I thought. There I was again.

SARAH

"I'm naked; put that thing away." I held up my hand to block the shot Hill was preparing to make. I couldn't remember him ever taking this many photos. Well, there had been that one time at my old place.

"Love the camera, babe." He straddled my hips, holding himself above me. A sight to behold was a very naked Hill with only a camera in his hands.

Why all the photos? Was he never coming back when he left this time? If gossip was right and Big Jack died soon, there was no reason for Hill to return. Who was he going to piss off? His mother? "Why?"

"Why what?"

"Why all the pictures?"

He lowered the camera so I lowered my arm. A faraway look came over his face as he stared at the wall. His grey eyes were dark like storm clouds. What the hell had happened to him on his last job? Something had. I wasn't an idiot. When he went some place particularly bad and saw horrible things through his camera then shared those pictures with the world, he always came back to Pierce Point.

He traced my mouth with a finger, then caressed down my throat, stopping over my heart. "You're so wondrously, beautifully alive," he answered in a low voice.

"Hill," I whispered.

"I need," a slow exhale made his shoulders rise and fall, "to see something vibrant and alive in my camera, Sarah, or I'll never touch it again."

I sat up and eased the camera from his hand. Gently, I set it aside. God help me if I damaged his precious toy. No, not a toy. It was his pen and paper. "What happened, Hill?"

"Hell. Hell happened and I was the asshole taking pictures of people suffering, of people mourning their loved ones, of people dying. There was this boy, he was maybe four, and he was all alone amongst all this death. And what did I do? I took his picture. What a hero. He was someone's baby and I was an asshole."

I flattened a hand over his heart. "Show me."

"What? Why do you want to see that shit?"

Because he had. And it was haunting him. I knew about ghosts. I had my own. "Show me, William."

He stared at me, then climbed off the bed. He crouched down beside his backpack, staring at it before he pulled out a small laptop. I retrieved his shirt, pulling it on as his computer made a bong powering up. After a few clicks on the trackpad, he handed me the laptop and walked away.

Sitting on the bed, I looked at the faces that were haunting him. I didn't know where he had been. Somewhere, anywhere, everywhere. Volcano? Mudslide? I didn't know. It was horrific. The defeated faces, the destroyed homes, the death. So much death. *Oh, Hill.* Then I found someone's baby. It made my heart thump hard to see that tiny body empty of life. He should be playing, laughing, throwing his arms around his mother in an enthusiastic hug. Instead he lay there with a few flecks of mud on his cheek, as if something had sent him flying above the disaster. An arm positioned wrong, a bare foot also splattered with mud. No blood, just…nothing but a shell.

I closed the computer and gasped for breath. Something hard twisted through me. Fear. Guilt. I grabbed the phone beside my bed and dialed. As the other end of the line rang, I knew this was a mistake. A horrible, horrible mistake. What was I going to say?

"Sarah?"

My breath caught in my chest at being caught. I hadn't talked to Donovan Riley in years. I had stopped taking his calls, the emails he sent were automatically deleted, and I returned any letters I received.

"Are you okay? Are you hurt?"

I shook my head as I thought of that small body. "No. I'm fine."

"Are you sure? You sound weird."

"I saw something. And it wasn't pretty." I ran my hand over Hill's computer. "I'm sorry I called."

Donovan was quiet. "Why did you? I'm glad you did. You've been avoiding me for years. It's pissing me off."

"Is…" No, this was so wrong. I had made promises. Promises to not ruin anyone else's life like I had trashed mine. And yet that picture. Somebody's baby.

"He's fine, Sarah," Donovan said in a quiet voice. "Napping. I can wake him up. Do you want to talk to him? You should, you know. He wants to talk to you."

"No." Shit. God damn, what would I do then? "No."

"Sarah…"

"Bye." I hung up, then turned off the ringer, knowing Donovan would call back. Because that's what nice guys did, even to women who had fucked up their lives, women who had put innocents in harm's way because they were selfish. Grabbing Hill's camera, I went looking for him and found him in the living room.

"I need alcohol." He was slouched on the couch, his eyes closed. Reaching out, I brushed my fingers over his short hair. He heaved a weary sigh. I wanted to wrap him up in my arms and protect him from this.

"Sorry. I got nothing." I sat down beside him and was surprised when he rested his head on my shoulder. This wasn't something we did. The most vulnerable we had ever been with each other was getting naked. I ran my finger over the side of the lens and made myself ease away from him. "What did you do after? When their stories were captured, what did you do? Can I guess? You put your camera back in your knapsack, set it in place and joined whomever was helping them. You scooped up somebody's baby and carried him out of the dirt. Maybe you found his mom, maybe you didn't, but I bet you looked for her. You dug out bodies; you probably handed out water."

"Huh."

Lifting the camera up, I aimed at his face. The camera was heavy and cool, but was an extension of Hill. Once he had taken his first batch of pictures, his camera had always been with him. He revealed truths with it, some harsh, some beautiful. "Tell me I'm wrong."

"You're wrong." He glared at me but I knew I was

right.

I took the picture and was sure it was out of focus. "Liar."

He took the camera and set it away. "You think you're so smart." He grabbed my arm and tugged so I sprawled across his lap. "That didn't keep me from being the asshole with a camera, Sarah."

"You told their story. You've shown them to the world so they won't be forgotten."

"I didn't send in the pictures. I couldn't. So you're wrong. I've done dick all."

Scooting up so I sat on his lap, I studied his gorgeous face. "Look at me, William." His lashes lifted as he met my gaze. "It's okay." A little whisper told me to lay my ghosts on the table too. Sharing with Hill scared me though. Too many disappointments fell into my lap because of him. This, whatever this that was happening right now, wasn't going to last. Because he would leave me again. He always left. It didn't matter that he came back because it was the leaving that killed little pieces inside me. And I had so few pieces left that I was clinging greedily to them.

As a teenager, I had been dazzled by Hill. It had taken a while for it to sink in that I was *not* in a relationship with handsome, bad boy Hill Deveraux. I was a stop. A port in the storm. One of many girls he'd fuck then leave.

And I wasn't strong so he'd come back, flinging scraps of attention at me. I had been starving for it, from him or anyone, so I had grabbed them until more and more of me had disappeared. Finally there had been nothing left. A bottle of flavored vodka and a packet of pills. One pill, one shot, one pill, one shot. Until there had been nothing left. No pills, no vodka, no Sarah. Just a crying baby who had deserved better.

There had been nothing accidental in my overdose. It hadn't been spontaneous, but meticulously planned out for years. After every beating I survived, every hangover I woke up to and every time I woke up emotionally wrung out from being me. I'd lie in my bed and plan it. A way out. A way to stop it all. Nothing that would hurt because I was tired of pain. Something simple, pain-free; drugs and alcohol were my method. All that had been missing was my rock bottom.

As I looked at Hill, I saw shadows of that sad, desperate hurt inside him. He was strong, stronger than me. "William Hilton Deveraux," I said quietly as I pressed my forehead against his. "You are not me."

With an inch between our eyes, I could see the black striations that made his eyes look darker at times. "You will not wake up and wonder what day it is, whose bed you're in, and reach for the open pill container on the nightstand." He sucked in his breath and rested his hands on my hips. "You're not going to drown in bottles. Because you're not me. So it's okay to shuck the armor and ghosts because they won't eat you up. Rage, mourn. It's okay to get lost in the storm. I know the way out," I whispered in his ear as I wrapped my arms around him. Strong arms banded around me and he pressed his face into my neck. I held him as long as he needed me to and when that wasn't enough for him, I gave him my body.

It was, I knew, the beginning of the end, because he would not let himself be vulnerable before anyone, especially me. He didn't want my love. It was a chain that held him to a place he hated. It was a tether to someone he didn't want. I called in sick. I gave him everything.

And in the morning he was gone.

Another piece died as I stared blankly at the spot where his duffle bag had been. "Hill Deveraux's whore," I whispered, pressing my face into his pillow.

chapter six

HILL

MY THUMB PRESSED the shutter, taking perhaps the umpteenth picture of rocks, and I wound to the next frame. Click, whir, click. "Damn, son, you picked a shitty ass day to phone me."

My shoulders twitched and I looked away from the angry water bashing the gravelly beach. My oldest brother, Jax, walked towards me, his hair misty from the overcast weather.

I went to wind to the next frame and was frustrated when I couldn't. Tilting my camera back, I discovered I had used up the twenty-four shots. I began to wind the film back into the canister. "You didn't have to come."

"Don't be stupid." Jax sat down on the beached log with names and dates carved into it. Somewhere on this piece of wood an angry, scared eighteen-year old kid had scratched his name into it. A way for everyone to remember I had been here after Big Jack had kicked me out. "You called. You *never* call."

Nope. I didn't. I pressed my thumb against the lock, the back of the camera popped open and I removed the film roll. There were photos of Sarah on here. Who was I kidding? There were photos of her in the bag between my feet. I could pop the top on all of them. Expose them. Turn them black. Then there would be no more photos of Sarah. "Still, you didn't have to come…here."

I had been the second one evicted from the family. Jax had been the first. His crime had been falling in love with Allison Durrand. Big Jack wanted to expand his Deveraux empire one fertile egg at a time. The egg, however, could *not*, absolutely not, come from the maid's beautiful daughter. Big Jack had threatened Jax: his money and future, or the girl. Jax had picked the girl, and just like that, his money for university had dried up, his architectural dreams had vanished…and so had the girl.

Their father was a clever bastard and knew how to fuck up lives. He had also given Allison a proposition: the boy or the money for her to go to Julliard to follow her dreams. She had picked the money and the future. Cold. Cold, cold, cold.

Bitch.

With Matt, my second brother, it had been the same thing because he had been in love with Molly Vale since junior high. There was nothing wrong with Molly unless one put worth on someone's bank account. And Big Jack sure as hell did that. He had issued the same ultimatum to Matt. Matt had picked the girl. This time the girl had picked Matt. They were still together.

Technically Matt hadn't been kicked out like Jax and I. He had walked away. That pretty much summed up my older brother. He may have been the jock in the family and built like a linebacker, but he was the calm brother. Aside from the general beating up on his younger brother, I only knew Matt to have thrown one punch in a fight.

And yet it was Jax I called, because I was drowning in my bullshit and my oldest brother had zero tolerance of bullshit. Especially mine. I needed that right now.

All three of us hadn't lived up to the level of excellence that Big Jack had wanted. He had tried to manipulate us all to be what he wanted and when that hadn't worked, his use for us was over.

"I'm thinking of visiting Big Jack," Jax said as he leaned forward, elbows on his knees.

"Bullshit." Maybe I'd just throw the film into the cove and let the salt water ruin it. I rubbed my thumb along the velvety lip. Visions of what would happen to those images of Sarah made my belly cramp. I found an empty plastic canister and carefully tucked it away. Protecting the film until I found a dark room. "Why would you do that?"

"He didn't win," Jax said softly. "He didn't win and it will piss him off knowing that. How is Sarah mine?"

My hand fisted on the film and I leaned back to shove it into his pocket. "Don't call her that." The chuckle from Jax said he knew he had scored a point. Asshole. "Fine. Sober."

"Really? Good for her. Did she say why?"

I shook my head slowly. No, she hadn't and I hadn't asked. I felt Jax staring at me and I fiddled with the camera. "What?"

"Still the little shit, Billy boy. I was going to drag your ass home with me to see Ally, but I think I'm going to leave you here so you can figure your shit out. You're twenty-fucking-six. Grow up."

Even though Big Jack had broken up Jax and Ally, he hadn't succeeded in the end. It had taken a few years and a lot of forgiveness, but Jax had married the girl. "You don't know shit."

"I know you're running," he said, nodding his head to the bag. "You come here for a reason. Why? To piss off Big Jack? To romp in Sarah mine's bed? To visit the glory days of being a Deveraux? Why? You're the only one of us who keeps coming back. Why?" He stood and I gazed up at my oldest brother. "Call me when you know."

I didn't want to figure out why I came back. That was something I wasn't sure I would ever be able to confront.

"How about a ride to the airport?"

Jax stared at me with cool grey eyes. He may wear a fancy suit while he drew fancy buildings, but there was no mistaking that beneath the civilized veneer he was still the big brother who had kicked my ass more than once. "How about you get a fucking clue? See you soon, son. Call me when you really need me."

"You're an asshole."

Jax lifted his hand in acknowledgement and walked toward a slick-looking Mercedes SUV. They were paying him way too much to draw buildings. Within minutes my ride out of Pierce Point was gone. So much for a rescue. So much for loyalty.

Deverauxs.

You just can't trust them when you need to.

SARAH

The last person I expected to find on my front step was Jax Deveraux. I blinked a few times. Yes, that was Jax with his short, dark blonde hair and tall, lanky strength. "Jax."

"Hello, Sarah mine."

My eyes filled with tears and I threw myself at him. Never in my wildest dreams had I expected a white knight to show up in my life. He had come to see me in the hospital, looking like some vengeful angel. Pissed. He had been so mad. Jax had been the one who paid for my time at rehab. There was one requirement: if I fell off the wagon within the first year, I had to pay him in full. For everything. Including the small personal loan that had gotten me out from above Brandi's and into my house. Every day he would phone: "Hello, Sarah mine. Are you sober today?" On the one-year anniversary of my sobriety, he had torn up the contract, hugged me, and walked away.

On my two-year sober-versary, as he called it, he had taken me into the Pierce Point cemetery. There he had shown me a modest marker that read Sarah Jane James October 15, 1989. "I found your next home," he said to me. "What do you think? A little smaller than your apartment but really, how much space will you take up?"

On my three-year sober-versary he gave me a job. He flew me from Vancouver Island to Toronto where I drew a sad five year old girl the bedroom of her dreams: a castle on one wall, a fairy garden on another, and in the clouds above her head, smiling images of the little girl's family that had been killed by a drunk driver.

Jax Deveraux was not subtle with his lessons.

"What are you doing here?"

He hugged me back, lifting me and walking me inside. "I ask myself that every time I come to this shit hole of a town. More importantly, what are *you* doing here?"

I shrugged as I let go of the man responsible for me being alive. If he hadn't come along I probably would've tried something far more successful. I had hit my bottom and saw no way out. Jax had helped me find a way out of my rock bottom.

He took off his coat and followed me into the living room. He tossed it on the armchair then pointed at me. "You've been crying."

"Well…you know."

"I can figure it out. Six-two, bit of a shit head, always has a camera in his hands? Did you tell him?"

"No." I sat on the couch and Jax sat in the chair, looking at me with a serious expression on his face. One that said he didn't want any of my excuses or bullshit. "No, I didn't. He's not going to care, Jax."

"Wow. You really don't think highly of my brother." Jax flicked a piece of lint off his slacks. "Good enough to fuck but not good enough to give your secrets to?"

"Hill doesn't want my secrets." He doesn't even want me.

Steel grey eyes pinned me to the couch. "Do not underestimate Hill, Sarah."

"He won't care. He doesn't. I'm the Pierce Point fuck. A girl in every port, right?" I fiddled with the hem of my jeans and wished there was something to drink.

Damn it.

"Perhaps at one point. I don't think there's been much porting going on with him. You need to tell him, Sarah. This is a small fucking town that thrives on gossip. Someone is going to tell him and it should come from you."

I shrugged. Hill was gone. What did it matter? "Are you threatening to tell him? You promised not to." Shit. What would I do if Jax picked Hill over me? I didn't have a lot of people on Team Sarah. Someone needed to be on my team or else I was going to smash apart. Pieces, pieces everywhere.

"And wasn't that a bad decision on my part? No, I won't tell him. *You* tell him. This is serious stuff, Sarah. He deserves to know."

Yeah, I thought as I looked away. No one on Team Sarah. "Right," I said softly. "So I can tell him I sobered up because I overdosed, and then what? What will he do, Jax? Stay? Suddenly, miraculously–" I swallowed my words.

"Love you?"

Wow, he didn't need to say it like it was impossible and improbable. I already knew that. Having Hill's oldest brother rub the fact that Hill would never love me in my face was not what I needed hours after waking up to find him gone. Yeah, I knew exactly where I belonged in Hill

Deveraux's life. And that was in bed, flat on my back. "Can you go? I'm tired."

Jax swore as I stood. "Damn it. Sarah—"

"I know where I fit in his life, Jax. I've known since I was fifteen years old and he treated me like a doormat to wipe his shitty boots on. I've known since I was seventeen and we had sex. Drunk or sober, I know exactly what I am to him, because he's not here, is he? Telling him what happened isn't going to change a thing. Do you know why?" I met his gaze, hating the tears that slipped free. "Because he still left. I know you came here for him and not me so go get him. He needs someone right now and he doesn't want it to be me."

Pressing my hand against my stomach, I walked into my studio and locked the door. I slid down the door, folded my arms over my head and did what I had vowed never to do again. I cried over Hill Deveraux.

Again.

HILL

What the hell was I doing? Dragging my hand down my face, I pressed the doorbell. I shouldn't be here. I should be trying to get as far away from Pierce Point as humanly possible. Jax wasn't the only means out. I found a ride at eighteen; I could find one at twenty-six.

Instead, I was standing on a familiar porch, ringing a doorbell. I had never, in all the years I had known Sarah, rung her doorbell. And didn't that just up my asshole quotient for the day.

The door opened and I stared in confusion. Why was Jax in Sarah's house?

"She's crying. Fix it."

I grabbed the front of my brother's shirt and shoved him hard against the interior wall. "And why, big brother, is she crying?"

Jax slapped off my grip then smoothed down the front of his expensive wool coat. "Well it sure as fuck isn't over me. Like I said, William, fix it."

I watched my brother walk down the sidewalk to his slick vehicle that I hadn't noticed before. Fuck. If Jax had hurt her, I was going to kill him. I was going to bloody up all that slick shit clothing Jax wore and make him hurt. I lowered my duffle bag and backpack to the floor then shut the door. I called out for her. "Sarah?"

Crouching down, I unlaced the battered hiking boots I had thrown on when I had slipped out this morning. They were easier to wear than carry. I looked up and Sarah stood there, tears still on her cheeks, her eyes red and puffy.

That was it.

Jax was dead.

"You left."

"I came back."

"You left."

Yeah. I had. Nodding, I stood up and toed off the heavy boots. "Just catching a head start on the kicking me out of your house." She nodded as she wiped impatiently at her cheek. "Got as far as the cove." I walked to her, nerves pricking at my skin. "Realized I had some unfinished business." Okay, had it shoved in my face but it was still a realization. It counted.

"Big Jack."

I shook my head as I cupped her face and gently brushed my thumbs over her eyes. "Sad Sarah."

She repeated the words and I nodded. I wanted to know why my brother had been here. Why the hell would Jax come see Sarah? My brother was ten years older than her and happily married to a woman I still didn't entirely trust to not rip his heart out a second time. Not that I suspected the two of them were having an affair. Jax knew Sarah was…

I mentally shrugged off the end of that sentence. But what the hell was going on?

"Why are you crying?"

"Do you really want to know?"

Searching her eyes, I rolled the question around in my head. When her lashes started to lower, I tilted her head up. I was getting damn tired of her always hiding from me. "No," I answered and saw the flinch in her eyelashes. "Because it probably means I hit the asshole bull's eye again." And wasn't that getting tiresome? "Unless it was Jax hitting the asshole button then I'll go kick his ass. Sure, I'll get a beat-down but I'll take the bastard down with me." I rubbed my thumb over her mouth, then met her teary gaze.

"You came back. You *never* come back."

What was she saying? Hadn't she been paying attention over the years? I *always* came back.

chapter seven

HILL

I TRACED THE graceful line of Sarah's spine. She was so damn beautiful as she lay on her bed, her body sated and soft. It was nice to know that even without her mind impaired by booze and drugs, Sarah Jane James was a sensual being. More so now, I decided, because she was right there with me. "You are," I said, leaning down to kiss the small of her back, "by far," I kissed the slight curve at her waist, "the sexiest woman," I gave the swell of her ass a bite and enjoyed the surprised gasp from her, "I know."

"Liar."

I lay down beside her. "No way," I said, kissing her shoulder. "I like knowing that even now you're getting all tingly and wet for me." Her snort made me smile. "Five bucks says you are." My hand glided over her ass and she shifted her leg to give me access. Her eyes closed as her mouth parted on a sigh when I found that she was wet

89

for me. "Tingly, Sarah?"

She nodded.

"Roll over." I leaned down, kissing her when she was right side up. Our tongues muffled her moans as she shifted, hips rolling in time to my caresses. There was something a little addicting in how she responded to me. Even that first night when she had been tipsy on her first beer and nervous about what was going on, she was right there with me. When I eased a finger into her, she cried out, arching up as she covered my hand with hers. Fuck, that was hot.

I knew exactly when she found what she was looking for because her slick walls squeezed on my fingers as she came with another cry. "So sexy," I said as I kissed down her arched neck, her fingers bumping mine. She reached up with her other hand and grabbed onto the pillow, as if that was the only thing holding her to the ground. With ease, she took a second finger, riding me as I found her swollen nipple waiting for me.

I throbbed to be back inside that oh-so-greedy, oh-so-generous body. Abandoning her breast, I ran my cheek down her stomach, feeling the muscles tightening and pulling with each needy roll of her hips. "Move it," I said, brushing her fingers. I smiled when she screamed, my tongue sliding over her. One more lick had her arching hard, squeezing my fingers and spilling over me.

"Oh so sexy," I said, sliding my fingers free.

Get inside her now.

It was my only thought as I brought her to orgasm again. "Hill." A hand pressed on my shoulder. Down? Up? I had a feeling she had no idea. Grinning, I looked up at her. And lost my breath. Her cheeks were flushed, her eyes closed though her lashes were fluttering. I grabbed her hand and slid it back where it had been. Rolling away from her, I grabbed my camera, then zoomed in on her face.

I waited, watching her through the viewfinder, her soft cries sliding over my skin like a touch. Not yet. Not yet. "Sarah."

"Don't you dare," she moaned.

Grinning, I shifted the shot and took it of her fingers. They flexed as her back bowed. Returning to her face, I caught the sensual image of her orgasm. I slid over her, unable to resist her anymore. As if I ever had.

"I hate you," she whispered as she lifted her head to kiss me. Slick fingers found me and I groaned as she stroked. "I hate you so much."

"No, you don't," I murmured as I let her guide me in. "Oh, no you don't."

"No," she moaned, her legs wrapping around my hips and she met my thrusts. "I really don't. Come inside me, Hill."

"Look at me when I do."

Her eyes opened and I stared into them as I did exactly as the lady requested. It was the least I could do.

SARAH

"Can I show you something?" I didn't look up from my sketchpad. What was I doing? There had always been fences with Hill. Places neither of us dared to go. I half expected to wake up and find him gone again. But he was still there, sprawled on my couch as he read a book, his jeans open at the waist.

Sexy man.

"Now?"

Frowning, I contemplated the question. If not now then it would be never. Nodding, I finally met his gaze. "Now." With a loud exhale, I set down my pad and pen, then stood up. The rubbing of his jeans over the couch cushions seemed loud to me as I walked down the hall, Hill following. "You showed me yours," I said as I gripped the doorknob. "This is mine."

Pushing the door open to the studio was one of the hardest things I had ever done. Because this was it. Jax was right. I needed to tell Hill what had happened because someone would tell him. The hell if I wanted Brandi to tell him out of spite.

It wasn't the fanciest studio, but then I wasn't the fanciest girl. Closing the door, I leaned against it as Hill gave the room a thorough look over.

Then he began to walk around. There were a few projects on the go because a few people I had met in rehab and I were putting together a show. Alistair Holt, who had once been pretty big in the Canadian art scene with his photography, had decided that it was time to return to what he saw as his slippery slope downward and had contacted me and the others about doing a show in Vancouver, centered around our addictions.

It was an opportunity of a lifetime and it terrified me. I was a bartender in a town of seven hundred people. No one knew. Not even Jax. "Don't look at that one yet!" I held out my hand, stopping him when he approached a long ream of paper on the floor. He had been quiet since he had walked in. "I need to…" I rubbed a hand over my heart, my stomach churning with fear and nerves.

He ignored me and crouched down, studying the drawing. He would know the table. It had been the coffee table in my old, shitty apartment. The paper was as long as the table had been. I knew what he would see. Inked renditions of empty pill containers, a tipped over vodka bottle with a little liquid still in the bottom. And an alternating pattern on the table. Pill, shot glass, pill, shot glass. There was a half empty wine glass and a baby's soother on the table. Two shot glasses were empty, two pills were gone.

He walked his fingers over the combination I had taken that night. His finger stopped over the empty spot. Slowly, he tapped it, then looked at me over his shoulder.

"Three years, one month, and three weeks ago," I said softly, "I took a lethal combination of vodka and ecstasy that sent me into a coma. By the time the air ambulance arrived, I had gone into cardiac arrest."

Hill shifted his finger and tapped the soother. He said nothing, just looked at me. Nodding, I gazed up at the ceiling. The white ceiling was easier to talk to than those grey eyes. "He's three. Lives with his dad. I'm pretty sure Donovan hasn't told him that when he was five weeks old, his mother sat on the floor of her crappy apartment while a cheap ass band played below and she overdosed right in front of him." Tears fell down my cheeks as I stared at the popcorn pattern on the ceiling. "Because who wants to know that, right? Who wants to know that their mother is so broken and dead on the inside that she'd rather die when she's supposed to love him and look after him? So I gave him to the one person who did love him and would look after him. Someone not fucked in the head, someone not broken, someone not afraid to live for him."

Hill stood up and stared at me. I wished he'd say

something. Anything. "I hated that they brought me back. Hated them all. I hated Donovan sitting beside my bed," my jaw began to hurt as I looked back at the ceiling. "I hated Billy, that's his name, for crying so loud that someone heard him down in the bar so they came investigating and found me. I hated the doctors. I hated them all because I just wanted it to stop, so I was planning what I'd do next when Jax appeared.

"He didn't leave when I told him to. He didn't leave when I screamed at him. He sat in that goddamn chair, his stupid pen always scratching over paper. "Sarah mine," he said, "it's been a shitty haul for you but suck it up, darlin'. This pity party has gone on long enough. You *will* get clean and sober. It *will* suck. But by God you will not let them win this way." Then he slapped a piece of paper in front of me that said he would pay for my rehab and give me a down payment on a house so I was not in that apartment. I don't know why I did it. Maybe because my own family never came to see me. I don't know. It was hell. It took a long time to stop hating everyone because I was alive. Then I stopped hating everyone. I began to draw again. I hadn't for years. One day I had a visitor at rehab and it was Jax. Told me he found what I needed and showed me pictures of my house….my home. That's what he called it. Sarah's home. I couldn't go back to that apartment, Hill. I couldn't go back," I whispered as I finally looked at him. He was staring at the floor, at the drawing.

"I saw you four years ago."

"Yeah," I whispered.

"Five weeks old you said?"

I nodded and he nodded too.

"Hey, Hill," he said without looking up from my sketch, "I'm pregnant." Finally he looked at me. "That would've been nice to know, Sarah. That would've been really fucking nice to know. But this…Jax. Jax knew."

Shit. I nodded again as he rubbed the back of his neck.

"My Jax?" He didn't see me nod. A bitter laugh escaped and made my stomach hurt. "That asshole. Asking me if I knew why you got clean, acting surprised when I said you were sober. That asshole knew. All along. Why am I just finding out now, Sarah?"

"I–"

"As opposed to three years, one month, and three weeks ago!" He yelled it out as he faced me. "What the fuck, Sarah?"

I swallowed and fought the urge to go to him. "Would you have come?"

"Fuck. You."

"Would you have come, William? Would you?" I was shouting too, fear that telling him was a bad idea.

"Be honest. Right now. Right here. In my room full of truths, would you have come if someone had said I had overdosed? Because between the bouts of all our fucking, there wasn't a lot of wondering about me. Even when you were here it was fuck Sarah, pretend she doesn't exist. Fuck Sarah, walk away. Fuck Sarah, walk away. No thoughts of me, no concerns. Just got an itch, let's see Sarah. Would you have come, William?"

"Yes," he shouted. "I always do. You will not lay all our shit on my door, Sarah. Because I'm pretty sure you were in that bed with me. I would have come and that's why you had Jax keep it a secret. You *died!* Sarah, you fucking died! Had someone called me to tell me you were in pretty bad shape, I'd have hauled my ass out of that jungle to get here."

My shoulders sagged as I looked at him. "No, Hill. You wouldn't have. I have to go to work." Not that I wanted to work. I just wanted to escape.

"No. This is not done. You are not running away. You must think I'm total shit to think that. Yeah, I'm selfish and was shitty to you, but give me some fucking credit, Sarah. You know me. Good, bad, and the asshole, you know me." He stalked across the room and lowered his face to mine. The storms were alive in his eyes: anger, fear, hurt. All because of me. "You know I would have come back for you. You think about that as you're pouring alcohol for that fucker who slapped you around. Because I *always* come back for you. Though at this moment I'm kind of asking myself why. Had you died would Jax call me? Or would I have found out knocking on your door a few nights ago? But I guess we'll never know. Fuck you for that, Sarah. Fuck you right back."

When my front door slammed behind him, I wondered if I'd ever see him again. As I walked over to the picture, I stared down at it. Jax's words that I'd underestimated Hill rippled around in my head, chased by the look in his eyes. I had hurt him. Badly.

Just once it would be nice to not fuck up my life. Once.

chapter eight

HILL

OVERDOSE.

Lethal combination.

Cardiac arrest.

The words banged around in my head and made my chest tighten. I stopped in the middle of her lawn, hands braced on my knees to catch my breath. I felt all wobbly from Sarah's words. I had seen her. I had been with her months before her OD. I should've seen something in her. Right?

"Breathe."

I shook my head as Jax appeared beside me, the hand on my neck was more welcome then I'd admit. I was mad at hell at him for keeping this from me, but so thankful I wasn't alone.

"She overdosed, Jacky."

"Yes, she did. Breathe, Billy. Breathe."

I sank down to my knees, gravity winning. "Was it

bad? Tell me."

"They lost her twice. Ten years of hard abuse had taken its toll on Sarah mine's heart and body."

Twice? Fuck. I lowered my head, bracing my forearms on her lawn. "Why didn't you call me?"

"She didn't want me to."

"You should've called me anyway." I'd have sauntered up to her door and found out from some stranger, or worse her damn sister, that she was dead. Nausea churned in my stomach. "You should've told me."

"I promised her. She was at the end of her rope, Hill. She had nothing left inside her. What do you think it would've done to her if I went against my word?"

"I had just seen her. She was… Tell me about the guy."

A sharp bark came from Jax. "You just learned she died and you want to know about the guy?"

I nodded. I wanted to know about the guy. Was he just another asshole who had used her and left? Like the asshole hyperventilating on her lawn?

"Not from around here. Prince George I think. Had a band. Shitty music. Decided they were going to tour the island, live like rock stars. From what I know, it was a short hook up. A couple of nights. He played at Brandi's. Helluva shock to both of them when he knocked her up."

I sat up, breathing a little easier now that I wasn't

imagining her dead on the floor of that shitty apartment. That drawing though…too real. Too real.

"He got points for not vanishing, but it's not like he was here all the time. He came over for the birth, visited more but I think it was too late."

My brother knew an awful lot about what had gone down. I could just imagine the mess Sarah's head had been when she learned she was pregnant. It was easy to bring up the Sarah I had once known. All skin and bones, big brown eyes that were so sad, lost and needy, spirit broken down from every damn person she came into contact with.

"She didn't tell me. Why didn't she tell me any of it? The baby. The OD. Fuck, Jax."

"Take a walk with me. I want to show you something. And I need you to muffle the ego. Would you have come, Hill?"

"Well, fuck you too." I was damn tired of being the asshole who would've left my…what? Would've left Sarah in the hospital.

"Not you now. You four years ago."

"Asshole." I jammed my hands in my pockets, walking beside Jax.

The me four years ago hadn't even noticed she was pregnant. I had watched her slide further and further down the rabbit hole with the booze and drugs and I had turned a blind eye, the thought pattern of 'not my problem' had grabbed me by the balls early on when the alcohol had gotten pretty noticeable. Even when I had left, I had seen her life snowballing out of control. Hadn't stopped me from fucking her. Would I, who had ignored every damn warning sign pointing at her head, have come back after turning a blind eye to everything leading up to her OD? I kicked a rock and nodded. "I'd have come back, Jackson," I said softly. For Sarah, I'd come back.

"You need to fix your shit, son," Jax said as he walked beside me, matching stride for stride. "Because this? This is the reality."

I blinked and looked around. My thoughts had distracted me and I had blindly followed Jax. The cemetery? Why were we…

I looked down and my knees buckled. Sarah Jane James.

"This is what chases her," Jax said, crouching down beside me. "It's not you; it's not her dickhead of a father. This." He tapped the flat headstone. It was simple. A soft grey color with her name carved into the marble. "It all stops here. If you can't step up and be someone she can rely on, you need to walk away. Permanently. No more rest stops between her pretty legs. No more knocking on her door when you decide it's time to piss on Big Jack's fire hydrant."

I flattened my hand on her name and knew my brother had done this. My brother's life lessons were not subtle. When I had first started with sexy fun times, Jax had taken me to the nearest hospital, parked me in front of the maternity ward door and said, "One day, son, this will all be yours. So glove up, little brother." I had gone beyond condoms. I had gone for a vasectomy. No way was I, in any shape or form, contributing to Big Jack's DNA cycle.

"You gave her a headstone? What kind of asshole does that?"

"The kind who does not want to see Sarah mine underneath it."

"Why? Why do you care what happens to her?" Frowning, I looked at my brother. "Why are you still here? You hate this place."

"Because you're my brother. Your shit is a mess, Hill, especially involving Sarah mine. And I sat my ass in the car, texting my wife because I knew Sarah mine was telling you what happened. I knew you'd run at that. That's what you do when things get tough." Jax stood up. "Figure it out, Hill. It's not that complicated. You need me, little brother, you call."

I nodded as I stared down at Sarah's name. "Jesus, Sarah." She had overdosed. She had damn near died on me. She had damn near left me alone. What the hell would I have done then? Who would I have then?

SARAH

Some nights, it just didn't pay to open the bar. I winced as tonight's band did some truly horrible things that should be illegal to classic Neil Diamond. Hill was mad at me. Not only had that ruined my day, but Alex Carson and his parade of idiots were in. Alex was a bully. He had been one in high school and he was one in his mid-twenties. Hill had been a bit of a jerk in high school and had made my early teen years hell, but he hadn't gotten any malicious pleasure out of it. Alex did.

Alex was the reason I had ended up with Hill in the first place that night in the cove. I had ventured out, not fitting in, no friends at my back, and Alex had seen me as prey. Had Hill not stepped in I would've wound up raped in the dark. I knew it. Hill had known it. Alex had said so. And he wouldn't have been the only one.

Until that night, he and Hill had been best friends.

I wasn't scared of Alex. At seventeen when he was threatening a gang rape? Yes. Now? Now, he was a twenty-six year old drunken excuse of a bully. Considering I had grown up in Brandon James' world, Alex was nothing.

Damon sidled up beside me. "Gonna be one of those

nights where you need to give me a raise."

Nodding, I watched Brandi sashay up to Alex's table.

"Subtle is not in your sister's vocabulary. She may as well just yank down her little skirt and flash the note on her ass that says "I'm having sex with a married man!" And a loser one at that." Damon rolled his eyes and walked off to cover his section of the bar.

No kidding. And I was called Hill Deveraux's whore? This town sucked.

The first order came in and from the annoyed look in my waitress' eyes, it was indeed going to be one of those nights. I should've called in sick for tonight too. With a screech of a guitar, the band moved on to murdering another song. It was so bad it took them reaching the chorus to find out what it was. Having one dude screaming into the microphone like a horror movie psycho while someone else abused the drums, and yet another advertising never having had a lesson on his guitar did not make for a fun night.

Tuesdays.

"Well, we can now let them know what day the music died."

Opening my eyes, I watched Hill sit down and look at the band. He was here? He hadn't left Pierce Point? My heart gave a few excited bumps to see him. He swiveled on his stool so he was facing me. "I didn't expect to see you." Tonight. Again. Ever.

"Yes, I know how highly you think of me."

With a sigh, I studied the angry man before me. "Right." I did not want to have to deal with this again. A part of me wanted to switch places with Damon but that felt too much like running away. "Can I get you a drink?"

"Coke." Then he spun his stool back around. At first I thought he was ignoring me but instead I saw he was looking at someone. Alex Carson. It wasn't a "hey buddy, how are ya" look. It was one that said he'd like to remove body parts.

"No fighting." Because that's exactly what the night was missing. Blood.

A grunt came from Hill and he leaned back, resting his elbows on the bar like he was some Western cowboy star. Oh God. There was going to be blood. Reaching over I flicked his ear. "I mean it, Hill. No fighting or I will throw your ass out."

He faced me again. "Little liar. You so want me to beat him up." He stared at me, that other night hanging between us. Did I want him to beat Alex Carson up? Hell yes. His lips curled up as if he knew what I was thinking. He folded his arms on the bar and leaned forward. His eyes focused on me and I fidgeted beneath his stare. "So tell me why there's a life-sized drawing of your old coffee table in your studio."

"Sarah, I need two Canadians and a red wine." The waitress had to yell over the music. Oh yeah, Tuesdays were awesome. It was as if my father put out ads for the worst possible bands. Ever.

"Minute," I said to him, then went to fill the order. When I returned, Hill's glass was half empty so I topped it up. Despite the amount of people in the bar, it wasn't overly busy. Mostly it was people who were bored or having affairs with married men when their wives were at choir practice. I knew, as did everyone else in the bar, that at some point Brandi and Alex were going to venture up to her soundproof apartment and have naked fun time.

Gross.

I had never done that with Hill. Okay once or twice there had been a quickie in the stairwell. Okay. Four times. Maybe six, tops. But we hadn't hurt anyone. No wives were humiliated, no marriages were at risk. And I was labeled the town slut. This town seriously sucked.

"What's wrong?"

I glared at Hill because he was safe. "Nothing."

"Says the woman glaring at me."

"Just thinking about things. Angry things." I shook my head. "So you want to know about the drawing?"

"No." Hill nudged his glass aside and braced his arms on the table, angling his body toward me so I could hear him over that stuff the band called music. "I want to know what's going on in your head. Because I'm pretty sure out of the two of us, I'm the mad one. Justifiably so."

With a sigh, I rested my arms on the table, duplicating him. "I'm thinking that double standards suck. *I* get called Hill Deveraux's whore and she," I jabbed a finger at my sister who was all but stripping for Alex, "sleeps with any penis that points at her *and* she's involved with a married man. I haven't had sex in four years but *I'm* the whore. That's what I'm mad about."

"Stop. Saying. That." His eyes were hard and that muscle was clenched in his jaw.

I shook my head. "I could become a nun...a fucking nun! And they'd still call me Hill Deveraux's whore."

He slammed his hand down on the smooth wood surface, startling those around them. "One more time, Sarah." He pointed a finger at me. "One more time."

"Or what, Hill? Or what? And *I'm* not calling myself that. *They* do." I flicked my hand toward all the people who came into *my* bar and judged me. They drank my booze and called me names. "Vicious, spiteful people."

"So leave. What the hell is keeping you here, Sarah?"

chapter
nine

SARAH

I STARED AT him and grabbed a cloth, wiping down my area. I couldn't look at him. I wouldn't. He would see and then he'd know. He would know why I stayed in this town that whispered about my mistakes behind my back and my family who treated me like the dirt garbage was piled on. And he could *not* know. He could never know.

That the reason why I stayed in this town was him. If I left, I knew he wouldn't come looking for me.

I glanced around and saw no one was paying us much attention. A few looks, a few whispers but that was all. "It's an art show."

"What?"

"The drawings. They're going in an art show." As a distraction, it was lame, but I didn't want him to start harping on me leaving because then what?

He sat up, his eyes wide. "Sarah, that's fantastic!" Was that pride? Blushing, I looked down. "Tell me. Lay it on me, baby."

I poured a few drinks then returned. "I met this guy in rehab. We had down time so I'd draw. It was crap, but I'd sit there and try to remember how to do things. This woman joined me. She painted. It grew. A bunch of us artsies, sitting around pretending we weren't addicts. There was this guy." When I looked up, Hill's eyes narrowed. What? Why was he mad? "He would sit with us, just sit. Watching us but never joining, but it was like he was with us, you know? Then a few months ago, I get this envelope from Cross Ties, that's where I was. I opened it up and there was this beautiful card. I'll show you when we get home. Anyway, it was this invitation to join in a show with the artsies. Shadow Self. That's what it's called."

"Tell me about this guy."

My eyebrows rose as he folded his arms on the table, his stare a touch violent. Really? I bit my lip to keep from smiling. "Older. Distinguished." Hill's brows lowered into a full on kill-the-beast glare. "A little heavy. Beautiful eyes." Maybe. If Hill asked me what color, I was going to have to wing it. I wobbled my hand back and forth. "Maybe early seventies?"

He sat up, the glower falling away. I grinned at him, refilled his drink, then took a few more orders. When Damon jerked his chin toward the tables, I followed his gaze and saw my sister, who was supposed to be working, straddling Alex's lap while they made out. For all I knew, the two were having sex right there since Brandi wore short little skirts to work. His friends hooted as if they were still in high school.

Hill looked to see what was going on. "Classy." His eyes rolled.

"Welcome to Brandi's on a Tuesday."

"Hm. And me without my camera."

"Liar."

His grin was a little evil. "Yes, yes I am. Do you think he'd get upset with me?"

Sighing, I pointed a finger at him. "No fighting." He grabbed my finger, rose up, kissed me, handed me his backpack, and wandered over to the pool tables. Shit. Damn it. I so didn't want to have to scrub blood off the floor. Even if it was Alex's.

Hill found a game, but I didn't believe his angelic face. At all.

Hill Deveraux and angelic were not in the same sentence.

Tuesdays. Freakin' Tuesdays.

HILL

The thing with growing up in a small town like

Pierce Point was that no one changed. The guys who had hovered around the pool tables when I was younger still hovered around. The girls who teased the boys still teased the boys. And the guys who were utter assholes were still utter assholes.

"So you're still taking those pictures?" Even though Avery Wilson and I had been in the same class all our lives, I wouldn't say we were friends. I tried to remember what Avery did.

Nodding, I watched Avery line up his shot. "You? Not up on the local gossip." Because I didn't give a rat's ass about the locals. Calling Sarah a whore? They could all just fuck off.

"Working for my father-in-law out in Victoria. It's a commute but can't afford to live there. He's got a print shop; I run the four-color press."

There wasn't much of an industry in Pierce Point. Small businesses for the most part. It was twenty minutes up the island from Victoria so everyone mostly worked in the city, some even in Vancouver. When I had been a kid, my father had closed the logging mill, and that had been the beginning of the end for Pierce Point. "Cool. You got a business card?" Avery finally scratched and I studied the table, calculating my best shot.

Nothing.

Jerk.

"Nah, but I'll give you the name of our sales gal if you want."

Nodding, I took a chance on a shot and scratched. "Thanks for that." As if I'd call. I took pictures. I didn't need to have things printed.

Avery grinned then leaned down, killing two balls in minutes. "Soooo…Sarah, eh?"

I looked at Sarah. She looked so wrong wearing the black shirt with her sister's name in hot pink on her breast. She had too much talent to be slinging beer for her bastard of a father. Resting the rubber end of my cue stick on the floor between my feet, I gripped the narrow tip and let it bear my weight. Did she know that the light in her eyes went a little dim when she was in here? I hadn't really caught on until she had mentioned the art show. Then happiness and excitement had sparked in those eyes. Maybe a hint of wonder that someone thought she was a good enough artist to invite into a show. She caught me staring at her and I winked. She made a face at me, winked in return before she went back to work.

Cute. She was so damn cute.

I turned my attention to the other man. "Here to play pool, Avery. Not going to talk about Sarah. A wise man would heed that." Because I would rip him apart. He had put on a few pounds over the years but that didn't matter.

Size was irrelevant because I fought dirty.

"Just making conversation."

"Just making a threat," I responded. My comment startled my former classmate enough that he botched his shot. My grin was a lot less pleasant as I took total pleasure in sinking three balls. "There are two topics of conversation that will turn this from a friendly game. The other's Big Jack. Make a mental note. Your shot."

I wasn't entirely sure if I meant the game or the idle mention of Sarah. Idle? I snorted as my gaze returned to Sarah. On my first night back, I had run into an older man I couldn't really remember who had informed me, as I started for the bar, that Sarah had moved. He hadn't even asked if I was looking for her. Address in hand, I had headed to where she was. In this place, even if I hadn't been about to knock on the wrong door, they'd assume I was crawling into Sarah's bed.

Where the hell else would I go when I returned? Why else would I return?

Hill Deveraux's whore.

That phrase Sarah dropped echoed through my head like a poisonous snake. Who the hell had said that phrase? She glanced my way again and I met her gaze, the pretty girl with the big, sad eyes. The broken girl who had shattered and had put her pieces back together. By herself. Yeah, my brother had helped but she had done it.

Brave, pretty girl who was stronger than she knew.

How could anyone not see that she wasn't that girl anymore? She didn't need the booze, or drugs, or sex to fill those empty holes anymore because she had filled them up on her own. However she had done it, she had done it. God damn, she was something. "Be right back." I walked across the bar, not breaking eye contact with her.

Walking around the end of the bar, I was well aware everyone was watching. Whispering. Let them. Fuck them all. What did they think I was going to do? Rip her jeans down and bend her over the bar? Mm, maybe. "Sarah James," I said as I backed her up against the counter behind the bar.

"What?"

I searched her eyes. "I have something to say to you." Her eyebrows rose before her lashes lowered. "No, no hiding. This is important shit that you need to hear." I waited patiently until she met my gaze. "You are amazing, Sarah Jane James. And I am humbled by how amazing you are." I kissed her. She smiled, then wrapped an arm around my neck, returning the hungry strokes of my tongue. "I'm so proud of you, baby." I kissed her nose, winked at her, and left her leaning against the counter, her cheeks flushed, her lashes lowered, and a little smile on her mouth.

"Aww," a snide voice said, "Hill and his whore having

a moment."

My wrist snapped out and I smashed the pool cue against Alex's chest. The man gagged, almost retching on his lap. Pity. That would've been fun to watch. The band halted mid-note. "We've had this discussion before, Alex. Don't make me remind you of the ending." I spun the cue up, resting it along my shoulders. As I stared down my former friend, Alex automatically swiped his tongue over the two fake teeth that replaced the ones I had knocked out a decade ago when Alex had said some shit about Sarah. My smile was sharp, lethal. When there was no rebuttal from Alex, I walked away.

"No blood, Sarah," I called to her as I joined Avery, who was looking a little pale. "Did I just lie to her?"

"No, no."

"Good. Your shot? I just had mine."

chapter ten

HILL

I WANTED TO rip up the drawing and set it on fire. I hated that it existed. I hated that it was so beautifully drawn so I could see the grains in the wood, the Brandi's logo on the shot glasses, and the stain on the carpet. That the table didn't rise up off the paper and put me in that crappy apartment was a miracle.

The soother. That damn soother. Somewhere in this world was a little boy who was half hers and half some asshole's named Donovan. Who named their kid Donovan? Rolling the camera lens from side to side, I wondered if he had Sarah's big brown eyes. Sarah had a son.

And she had overdosed. Exhaling loudly, I looked at the sketches scattered around the room. Because I hated this one, this evidence that she had damn near died on me, I stood up and walked the room. There was one of a little girl's bed, black snakes slithering out from underneath it and crawling up walls. *Sarah.*

One stopped me cold. Just looking at it made me feel clammy and nauseous. Intricately drawn rocks dominated the picture but they weren't the focal point. There was an empty plastic cup, and in the background were two shadow figures. They weren't precise and there were no details, just black lines that formed two bodies. Subtle, sneaky. A male over a female. It was in the arch of her back, the slight rise of breasts. Two shadow bodies. Male. Female.

Me. That was me. I knew it. Down to my bare, cold toes I knew that was us that first night.

Shadow self.

"Hill?"

I stared at the rendition of me, at the cup, at the overdose table. *Shadow self.* I walked back to the snake drawing, leaning over it as I looked. Really looked.

"What are you doing?"

Looking. Seeing. There she was. It looked like the shadow of a curtain until one saw it wasn't fabric but a leg, an arm, a head bent over as if she was hiding from the snakes coming for her. I continued to study the drawing because…there. Under the dresser. A camera lens. Fuck. Jesus. I couldn't breath as I really looked at her drawings. Finding her, finding bits of me. A camera here, a camera lens there, shadowed sex figures in another.

Wiping my mouth because I was pretty sure I was

going to throw up, I stared down at that goddamn table drawing. Looking for her. It became an obsession to find her in this one, the homage to what had stopped her heart twice. "Show me. Fucking show me." Because I couldn't find her. I couldn't find her at all in this one. Reaching up, I grabbed her wrist and pulled her down. "Show me. You show me, goddamn it."

Tears fell down her cheeks as she pressed her free hand to her mouth.

Her hand was shaking as she pointed. I didn't care about the camera. Fuck the symbolism of me in this. Yeah, I got it. I was part of the shit in her life. I was part of the problem. Hadn't she said so the other day? What I so desperately needed to know was: where the hell was she?

"Where. Are. You?" I jabbed my finger toward the drawing as I glared at her. A broken sob came from her. I knew her tells. Hell no.

I couldn't find her because she wasn't in there. No Sarah. And it freaked me out. "You put you in there, Sarah. Right now. Right now, goddamn it!"

She shook her head slowly and I stood up, heading over to the neatly organized counter. Upending a cup, I grabbed one of the ultra fine tip markers she liked. She was bent over, crying. "You put you in there, Sarah." I took off the cap and put the pen in her hand. Fuck, my hand was shaking. "You will go in there. I don't care where, but you put yourself in there, Sarah." That table had stopped her heart. Stopped it. Dead. Twice. I needed her in there.

I needed to know that in this macabre table where she had hatched out her overdose that she was in there. "I will burn this bastard to ashes if you don't put yourself in it." I sounded like an idiot, yelling at her over this but it didn't feel ridiculous. I knelt in front of her and caught her arms, dragging her up so she was kneeling. Tears fell, her nose was running, and heart-breaking sobs made her body jerk.

"Please," I whispered as I cupped her face, my voice shaking. My body was shaking. "Please, Sarah. You need to be in it, baby. I need you in there. Please, Sarah." I pressed my forehead against hers. "You will not leave me all alone in that nightmare of a picture, Sarah. You will not leave yourself out."

She gripped my neck and I kissed her, needing physical proof she was alive. My brother had somehow found a way to help her out of the shadows because I hadn't.

She had died. In that fucking picture she had died. *That's* why there was no shadow Sarah hidden in it.

"Please, baby," I whispered, wiping her cheeks as I found her mouth again. When I looked at that drawing, I needed to see her. Needed to find something of her in it. I got that it was all her, but I wasn't feeling very rational at the moment. I needed her in that picture somewhere.

Even though she was in front of me and I was touching her, I needed proof in that picture that she had survived. Lowering her to the floor, I didn't break contact with her mouth. As if I'd fall apart somehow. "You tried to leave me, Sarah."

"I tried to leave me."

"Don't," I said as I buried myself deep into her, causing her to cry out as she wasn't entirely ready for me, "do it again." There was nothing gentle in me, in this room filled with her demons, and I tried to be gentle with her but Sarah was having none of that. Her legs hooked over mine as she drew my head down, kissing me with the same desperation clawing at my belly. I rolled away from the drawing, so she was above me. *Sarah.*

Holding her head to mine because I couldn't release her mouth for any length of time, I tried to watch her ride me. That was always a sight to behold. Her eyes closed, her body rolling and rocking to her sensual pace. There was nothing sensual about this. It was raw. It was a sexual frenzy. As if she needed to feel as alive as much as I did.

It wasn't angry; we had done that before. This wasn't a battle. This was need. Simple, basic.

Complicated.

When she came, I flipped her to the floor, a little sorry that this was on a hard floor. Not that sorry as I plunged and took until she cried out my name as she came again. I couldn't have stopped my own orgasm if I tried. And I didn't.

We lay there, gasping for breath and I shifted them so I was beneath her again. "Sarah," I said softly as I brushed her hair out of her face. She rose up, then with a sigh, kissed me.

Sarah mine.

HILL

The house was big and ostentatious. A blatant shout of "I have money and you've got shit."

I hated it. Everyone had thought growing up a Deveraux had to be fantastic. Money, power, position, wealth. Ha. What the hell did they know? The only one in the house who had any of that was Big Jack. I had had nothing. I had been the third son, yet another cog in the Deveraux genetic wheel. Evidence that Big Jack had sperm to land not one but three male heirs. Like that meant anything these days. God help us all, if one of us had been a girl.

Big Jack saw Pierce Point as his empire. He was a Deveraux so that made him king. I was his son and that meant I was a prince, destined to inherit all of this with my brothers. Only none of us had fit the mold Big Jack had built. Jax had been the quiet, artsy one. The romantic one–with granite fists. Matt had been the athlete: smart, tough. Had our childhood not been so restrictive, perhaps Matt would've followed in Big Jack's footsteps.

And me.

Who had I been?

Nothing. No one special. The youngest who had no real ambitions aside from getting into as many pairs of panties as I could, the aimless one until the day I picked up a camera for a school project. Then shit had fallen into place for me because I was good at it. I hadn't joined the school paper and wandered around taking pictures of school spirit and shit, but I had taken pictures. I learned about lighting and timing and everything necessary to capture a piece of time.

Big Jack hadn't liked that at all.

If he couldn't control it, if it wasn't under his power, Big Jack hated it. That his sons had dared to find what they loved beyond Big Jack? Not allowed.

Had I not been as selfish as I had been, what would've happened to me had I caved to my father's demands? Stuck here, hating my life, hating everyone because I was trapped. I'd have turned into a miserable bastard like my father. Hurting people because I could, manipulating because the power was in my hand.

I may not be the best person on the planet but I sure

as hell wasn't my father.

I climbed the low steps and rang the doorbell. The door was opened by someone I didn't know. Did they know me? Whatever. "I'm here to see Big Jack."

"He's…"

"Dying. Don't give a shit." I shouldered my way in, set my duffel bag down, then pointed toward the staircase. "Upstairs?"

"Sir…"

"Call me Hill. This won't take long. Truthfully, you can continue to hold the door. I will be that fast." At least my father couldn't put his hand around my throat and throw me out again. I took the stairs two at a time. Not much had changed. It still stank of money and pride and greed. The walls had changed color but that was about it. Not that I cared about the décor. A feminine gasp made me look as my mother walked out of a room. She was older. Her hair short, a silvery grey now rather than the pale blonde I remembered. She was still elegant, still regal. Did she still smell of expensive perfume? I should feel something because this was my mother. She had given birth to me.

"William?"

She was the type of woman my father had wanted me to marry. The daughter of money, the perfect society bride who knew how to walk the walk and talk the talk.

The total opposite of Sarah.

Thank.

God.

I nodded as I adjusted my backpack on my shoulder, continuing to the other door. That my parents had created three children was a miracle. They didn't share a room. According to Jax, they never had. They had gotten together long enough to procreate, to meld their superior DNA into three inferior sons.

I opened the door and stopped. Stared.

There was an oxygen tank pumping the big O_2 through a tube; another bag hung by the bed spilling something into Big Jack's veins. It smelled like a hospital: medicinal, sickly, deathly. The father who had stood so tall, proud and smug in his power suits was a shadow of himself. Dying. Because not even Big Jack's money could buy off the cancer eating him alive.

"Now's not a good time, William," my mother said, without any sadness in her voice. Would she mourn him, her husband of forty-six years? Or would she feel free?

"It's the perfect time."

My father's eyes opened at my voice. He frowned. "William?"

I nodded as I studied the dying man. Should I feel something? Remorse? Anger? I had been so pissed at Big Jack for years that it was surprising to not feel it now.

Death—the great equalizer. The best thing that had ever happened to me was being kicked out of this family. This broken, dysfunctional excuse of a family. Because had I stayed and become what Big Jack wanted, I'd have turned into a miserable, selfish son of a bitch.

"You're not welcome here."

Ahh, there the bastard was. Yep, definitely no television death bed reunion show here. "Oh, I know. Thank God for that." I crouched down and rested my arm on the mattress. "I have something to say to you. Jax, you remember him, right? Your eldest? Asked me why I kept coming back here. Being the blight on your empire was a benefit but you know the real reason? And I kinda just figured this out." I leaned forward and lowered my voice to a whisper: "I pickedNow the inappropriate girl too."

Standing up, I hitched the bag up my shoulder. "Mother." I nodded at her before I walked away. Big Jack shouted my name.

Just like when I was eighteen again. I grabbed my duffle bag where it waited at the door and I didn't look back as I walked out the door.

Free.

The word whispered and wound its way through my head. I understood what Jax had said about wanting to see Big Jack. My father hadn't won.

Free.

SARAH

I opened my eyes and saw Hill's spot was empty. Rising up on my elbows, I looked to the spot where his bag had been. Gone.

Again.

Left behind.

Again.

"Damn you, William."

With a tired, defeated sigh, I lay down and stared at where he was supposed to be. Had I really thought he'd stay? Well, no. But I hadn't thought he'd sneak away when I was sleeping. Just once…

Just once I wanted him to tell me good-bye. To look me in the eye before he left me behind. Maybe he'd give me a kiss good-bye. Something, anything but disappearing on me while I slept.

I knew this time was it. There would be no miraculous return to my door. Hill Deveraux had breezed into Pierce Point like the emotional storm he was and had swept right back out.

Hadn't I known this would happen?

What? That because I was sober and things had been utterly different that things would change? Really?

I climbed out of bed and contemplated stripping the sheets. Not yet.

I grabbed my robe and headed for the shower when

I saw the studio door was open and the lights were on. Curious, I walked in to see the stool in front of the OD drawing. It had not been there early this morning when he had scooped me up and carried me into my bedroom.

My black marker sat on the stool and I knew what it was for. To put myself in there. I picked it up and saw a piece of paper torn from my sketchbook. Bold strokes formed my name.

Sarah—I'd have come. I will always come. I'll be back for this. Hill.

This? Looking down I saw his camera sitting on the drawing and my heart gave a ridiculously excited thump. Picking it up, I held it against my chest. Frowning, I leaned forward and studied the edge of the table. Now that had absolutely not been there before. He had printed in small letters: Sarah Mine.

"Damn you, William. That's vandalism." I pressed my mouth against the cool metal of his camera and smiled.

He was coming back.

Sarah mine.

He was coming back...*for me.*

chapter eleven

HILL

I ROLLED THE lens between my palms, missing my camera. It took me a few panicky heartbeats to remember it was with Sarah whenever I reached into my bag of tricks for it. Impulse had made me leave my beloved camera with her. Something I kind of wished I hadn't done.

I missed my camera, the comforting weight of it in my hands. That camera was an extension of me; hell, it *was* me. That's why I had left it with her. So she'd know I'd come back and that she wasn't alone.

I had screwed up a lot with her in the past. I had let her down, and not just on that day she had decided to pop deadly pills and drink shots of vodka. Since I had let Brandi manipulate me into teasing and mocking her shy, artistic, and already beaten down sister, I had been letting Sarah down.

What a dick.

The shiny vehicle that turned into the driveway made me look up before I stared back at the lens. My big brother was right. I needed to get my shit together. Watching Sarah slowly pull herself together, laying her demons out on paper for the world to see, made me feel like a coward. There she was showing everyone what her choices had cost her, including her baby, and what was I doing? Licking my wounds and hiding under blankets.

The slamming of car doors made me watch Jax and Ally. I didn't trust my sister-in-law but Jax loved her. I wasn't sure I could trust someone who had done what she had. Maybe my brother was a better man than I. While Ally took my sleeping almost eighteen-month-old niece from the back, Jax took out the baby carrier with two month old Elise. There was a certain amount of irony that my brothers had both had girls.

"Hello, Hill," Ally said in her soft voice. She knew I wasn't her biggest fan.

"Hey, Ally. How was rehearsal?"

She blinked in surprise. Could've been because I knew that's where they had been or because I had asked. "It was good. Would you like to come to the performance on Monday?"

Classical music wasn't my bag. I gazed up at the woman my brother had sacrificed everything for. Her hair was a soft golden color and her green eyes often reminded me of a cat. There was something classically beautiful about Ally. I could easily see her in the lens of my camera, looking at her daughters or playing the violin. Nodding, I rolled the lens. "I'd like that."

She beamed a smile then eased around me. "Sorry, I've got to get her down. She is no lightweight anymore."

Standing up, I took the key from her hand and opened the door. I left the key in the lock as Ally made her way into the house Jax had designed for them years and years ago when they had been teens in love. A few years ago he had finally built it for her. My brother knew his shit when it came to designing a house. It was gorgeous. A kind of a log cabin with large windows.

"Damn, son," my brother said softly. "You look fucked over. Beer?"

"Yeah." I sat back down on the step and Jax set the carrier down, giving me a view of the newest Deveraux. Cute little bug with all her fair hair and little mouth puckered. "You're going to look like your mama, aren't you?" Reaching out, I caressed the little cheek and wondered about Sarah's little boy.

A few minutes later, Jax returned carrying two bottles of beer. He sat down, snapped open the restraints that held Elise in, then stretched out his legs.

"Saw the old man," I said as I twisted off the cap.

"Shut the fuck up."

With a grunt I took a sip of the beer. "First time I've seen him since."

"And?"

"He's dying." That made me sigh, then I tilted the bottle back. "Hasn't changed even now."

"Did you think he would?"

No, not really. I didn't want to talk about Big Jack. We both knew our father was a selfish bastard. Old news. "How'd you and Ally get past all your shit? How were you able to forgive her? What did she have to do?"

My brother was quiet as he sipped his beer and looked at his daughter. There was a little tug of envy that my brother had all this. Then again my brother wasn't the complete shit I was. "Groveled. She groveled. A lot. Begged me for forgiveness. Then gave me a blowjob."

I coughed, choking on my beer. My brother's grin was a little evil and I wondered if there wasn't some truth to that line of crap. Somehow I didn't think Sarah giving me a blowjob would make up for all my shit. Blinking, I stared blankly at the neatly cut lawn. But it would sure be fun to give it a try.

"I let it go," Jax said softly. "Let it go, Hill. You're not the same guy you were, just like Sarah isn't the same girl."

It wasn't surprising my brother had jumped on the Sarah train. What other ride was there in my life? "I was a dick to her."

"So? She's never held it against you. Much. It's never made her shut the door in your face for good. You're not as much a fuck up as you think you are, kid."

I grunted as I set the bottle down and fiddled with the lens. I missed my camera. There were digital cameras in my bag but they weren't *my* camera. "She's in an art show."

Jax lowered the bottle he had just lifted to his mouth. "Shut up. Good for Sarah mine."

Turning my head, I looked at my brother. "Do not call her that."

"Why?"

"Because she's *mine*."

"Yes, she is," Jax said with a shit-eating grin. He tapped the neck of his bottle against the lens I held. "Yes, she is. So why then are you on my front step and not hers?"

Because I needed to get my shit together. Starting here. I reached into my backpack and pulled out the laptop. Flipping it open, I handed it to Jax. The photo program was already running and when the computer woke fully, the horrific image of somebody's baby took up the screen.

"Fuck, Billy," my brother whispered. Automatically, Jax reached over to touch Elise then looked over his shoulder as if that would make Ava magically appear.

"This what chased your ass to Sarah's door?"

Nodding, I reached down for my beer. Maybe a miracle would happen and my bottle would be full. Empty. Fuck. I fiddled with the lens instead, twisting the settings around. Finally I set it down and pulled out one of my digital cameras. It was better than nothing in my hands. I really wanted my camera.

I captured Elise in the screen and caught her sleeping. Alive. Frowning, I fiddled with the camera. I missed the bulk of my old camera. The way I had to think about things so I didn't waste a shot. This point and click was not for me. There was nothing to distract me.

"Damn, son."

"I never sent it in. I couldn't," I admitted. "What the hell am I doing, Jax? What good can possibly come from anyone seeing that photo?"

"Nothing," Jax said in a soft voice. "Isn't that the point, Hill? You don't take feel good pictures. You never did. But they're honest. I am terrified of something happening to my girls. As I looked at that photo you know what I thought?"

I shrugged as I pointed the camera at the step, the shadow of my leg and Jax's beside it. Artsy, but I still took the photo.

"Thank fuck. Thank fuck that's not Ava or Elise. Or Matt's girls. I know where my girls are; I know they're sleeping safe in this world that isn't always nice. I should probably be less selfish and mourn for that boy's family, but I can only think of mine. You see that stuff, Hill. You've always looked for images that make people stop, stare, then give thanks that's not them. That's what you're doing, Hill."

Tilting the camera, I aimed the lens at my brother. In the small screen on the back, I could see the lines of my brother's face. Different yet similar in some ways to mine. Marks of being half Deveraux and half Hilton. Family. I took the picture then returned to fidgeting with the camera. "So what you're saying is that I'm taking pictures of people's tragedies to remind myself that's not me?"

Jax shrugged. "Maybe. You were barely a kid when Big Jack kicked you out. I think you needed some reminders that things could've been a lot worse for you. Let's face it, you got talent but you also got luck. How many eighteen-year-olds with nothing but a couple of changes of clothes and a camera wind up where you are? Look at you, Mr. Hot Shot Photojournalist. Look at what you fucking did with your life."

Grunting, I hit the power button on the digital camera, watching the lens open and rise out then slither back in. I missed my real camera, the simplicity of it. "You think I should send it to my editor. Don't you?"

"What scares you about that picture, Hill? What

brought you to a full-blown stop and sent you seeking salvation with Sarah?"

My heart thumped as I fiddled with the shooting mode dial. My brother sat beside me, his shoulder brushing mine in a comforting way. "You just said that it made you–"

"Nope. Not talking about me, son. Belly up to my truth bar, kid. What scared you?"

A slow, heavy sigh escaped. "Me. I'm tired of seeing dead babies, dead women, dead men, dead civilizations, dead lands, dead. Everything dead."

Jax pointed over his shoulder. "Right there. Take the picture. Right now."

I turned to watch Elise's nose wrinkle, a little squawk and a yawn. Dark lashes lifted and sleepy grey eyes looked at the world. Deveraux eyes. My hand shook a little, and I took the picture as she gave a little bounce at seeing her dad. Pretty little girl who was far from the machinations of the grandfather who would discount her because she was a girl.

"Now there's a baby alive on your camera. And let's face it, there's nothing prettier than one of my girls. You need to start taking some feel-good images again, Hill. I'm not saying set up shop and take pictures of flowers all day, but you have to remember the light after you see the dark. It's why you go back to Sarah. She's alive, she's living."

She was light. I watched my niece discover her hand and chew on it, utterly content to show off her skills to her proud daddy.

"Why'd you pick that house for Sarah?" Resting my elbows on my knees, I stared through the viewfinder again, ignoring the screen at the back that would show me the photo. Cheating, I thought, as I took in the house across the street. Matt's house. There were three houses on this street, only three. The other two Deveraux boys had done well for themselves without Big Jack's money, maybe even in spite of it.

Matt's house was different than Jax's cabin and glass home.

It was large and bright. Evidence of little girls was on the lawn: a little pink bike, a red ball, glass butterflies in the garden that Molly had created in the front. Lucky bastards.

Jax sighed and took a sip of his beer. "Because if she went back to that apartment after rehab, I don't think she'd have made it. She didn't need ghosts to welcome her home. It was a fresh start."

Pretty pictures, I thought. Pretty images that didn't remind her of the shit in her life.

"Why there? Why not here or anywhere else in the country?"

Jax's hand blocked the shot and he lowered the camera. "You tell me, William? Why would Sarah stay in Pierce Point? Your head seems to be firmly out of your ass; why would she stay there?"

I clasped my hands behind my head as a heavy sigh escaped. "Me. Even after all the shit I've put her through?"

"Even after all the shit. Ask me your first question again, Billy."

"How were you able to forgive Ally?"

My brother stood up and squeezed my hand. "Same way Sarah is able to forgive you, kid. Come inside, Hill. Time to stop running. And stop giving my wife shit for her mistakes or I will take you down." Jax snagged the handle to the carrier and walked inside, the front door open behind him.

Switching the camera setting to view mode, I panned back a few pictures and stared down at the headstone. My thumb hovered then I hit the delete button. The previous photo was Sarah lying in her bed, asleep as she had been that morning. She had my camera. I was going to go back for it. It was my lifeline.

Just like her. I powered off the camera, grabbed my bag and followed my big brother inside. If anyone could help me get my shit together, it was going to be Jax. Fixing my life was, after all, his hobby.

This was going to suck.

Jax's life lessons always did.

chapter twelve

SARAH

I FELT A little nauseous as I followed the tidy sidewalk to the door. Nerves were a powerful thing. Before I could ring the doorbell, I spotted the note that said to use the back door. With a little sigh of exhaustion, I walked around the side of the house. I could hear the water and there was a tug of envy. Even though I lived in a town along the Georgia Strait, I didn't get to see the water. This house way on the other side of the strait had one hell of a view.

The deck was monstrous. Huge. Oh, what I could do with a view like this. It was way more inspiring than the one of my fence. Every morning I could sit on the railing and draw. I yearned for this view.

When I looked away, I saw the bare feet first. Crossed at the ankles and resting on the railing. That's when I knew.

Sneaky Deverauxs.

Hill was sprawled in a chair, watching me, his camera aimed at me. The camera I had forgotten about because of nerves. Very sneaky. "You broke into my house?"

"Breaking and entering is such a harsh term. Did you know Jax had a key?"

No, I hadn't known that. Sneaky Deverauxs. "Is there even a barbecue?"

I had known when Jax had casually mentioned a barbecue that I would see Hill. There was a fine line between what I was more nervous about: seeing him or being part of the art show.

His lips curled in the bad boy grin I knew so well. "Of course. Smile, baby." Even from the slight distance between us, I heard the shutter click as I glanced down. He lowered his feet and uncurled from his slouch. As he walked toward me, my heartbeat grew a little faster and a little louder. "*That* is really annoying. Hi," he said as his hand cupped the back of my head and he gave me a slow, thorough kiss that left me breathless.

"Hi," I whispered back. He looked good. He had gotten a hair cut and his eyes didn't look haunted. I caressed his cheek then rose up on my toes to kiss him again. "Sneaky, William. Very sneaky."

He smiled against my mouth. "I have my moments."

I smacked his shoulder then impulsively threw my arms around him. "I missed you," I whispered, half afraid to vocalize my feelings. But I had. Every day since he had left his camera behind, I had missed him, looking for his stupid boots resting on my railing. Two months, I thought. Two long months.

No phone calls, no emails, nothing but that camera telling me he'd be back. Not for the camera. For me. Arms wrapped around me, holding me close. Maybe, just maybe, he had missed me too. The thought made me smile even as my heart fluttered nervously.

"I had some things to do. I sent the pictures in," he said. "I thought about what you said, and Jax is always good for bossing me around. I sent them in, because *he* deserved more than to stay on my laptop."

I nodded, rubbing his back, knowing Jax wasn't the *he* Hill was referring to. It didn't surprise me that he had done something with his photos. "Good."

"I turned down another assignment though. I had some shit to do. Can I show you?"

Nodding, I let him take my hand, and we walked into the house. It was a little bare furniture-wise. A couple of bar stools at the breakfast counter, a leather couch with a coffee table covered in photos. "Those are yours," I said as I caught a glimpse of the pictures. I studied the pictures.

"Yes."

I picked up a picture, my eyebrow rising because it was a photo of me. One he had taken of me undressing.

They were, I realized, all of me, except one. It was an iron sign arching over a gate, a declaration of ownership while saying keep out. I ran my finger over the name Deveraux. "I went to the funeral."

"Why?"

Jax had been there too. A quiet figure sitting on a pew who watched and listened to them talk about the great things Big Jack Deveraux had done. There was no greatness in the man. "Because he's dead and he can't hurt you anymore. Any of you."

"Sarah," he said softly, pressing his lips against the back of my neck. "I thought of going. Nothing good would have come of it."

"No more *fuck you* to him?"

"No more. He's not worth it."

I turned to face him. "You really *did* get your shit together didn't you? Did William Hilton Deveraux grow up on me?" He grinned and gave me a kiss, before he plucked the photo away and tossed it back onto the table. Then he pinched my ass.

"No."

"Oh, thank God."

There were boxes stacked up against the wall. All of them were titled and dated. I recognized the locations from some of his shoots. Were those boxes filled with photos? Some framed photos of little girls were on the wall. I recognized Ava and Elise, and assumed the other girls were Matt's. That made me smile. He had family pictures up.

"This used to be Jax's place," Hill said, heading downstairs. His fingers entwined with mine. "Before the new house was finished." He turned and leaned his back against a door. "He's letting me rent while the paperwork goes through. It's going to be mine."

A home. He had a home. Leaning forward, I lightly kissed him. "No more hotels?" I wondered if that had always been Jax's plan: to give his wayward younger brother a home. Considering the way Jax could plan, I had no doubt.

"No more hotels. I need a place to…come back to."

That made my heart clench. Not my place?

"So I've spent the past couple of weeks getting to know my brothers again. I've got some pretty cool sisters too. Mostly, though, I've been getting my shit together. This used to be the family room," he said softly, staring at me. "I've made a few changes. I took away some of the square footage and put in a dark room. But I realized something when I was with you."

I liked that he had a dark room. I liked that a lot. But he would come back here and not to me. "What?"

"You need more light, Sarah mine." He twisted the doorknob and his weight on the door swung open. I stared. The view. The wall was all window and looked out at that water view he had on the deck. The other walls were a soft yellow, the hardwood floors were stained dark and glistened under the lights. A sketchbook sat on the floor and I walked over to it. It was the same one I used; a box of the markers I preferred sat on top. Both were new. It was so easy to imagine my studio in here. There was a door across the room with a light above it. His dark room. And this, I thought as my heart pounded hard and fast with excitement, was *my* studio.

He stood behind me, a warm presence at my back. "I told you," he whispered against my ear, "I would come for you."

This was overwhelming. Reaching up, I gripped his forearms as I leaned against him, gazing out the windows to his impressive view. "This is for me?"

"Just like the barbecue tonight. I once asked you why you didn't leave Pierce Point if you're so unhappy there. Why? Tell me why, Sarah?"

I turned away from the water. He had seen my demons laid out on my studio floor. He had shown me his with that photo. I always knew when something bad was going to show up in a magazine or newspaper, because Hill showed up at my door. Reaching up, I traced his eyebrow. "How would you find me if I wasn't there?" I met his gaze and took a deep breath. "Would you even try?"

He sighed. "You gotta stop assuming I'm a total ass-hole, Sarah. It's hell on our relationship."

The word made something tighten in my chest as I focused on his chin. "Is that what we have?"

His hands gripped my hips and he lowered his forehead to rest against mine. "Sarah," he said softly. "You're about to show the world the shadows in your eyes, ones I helped put there. Stop hiding from *me*. You know all my shit, more than anyone on this planet. So, why are you always hiding you from me?"

Because he had the power to hurt me in ways no one could. I plucked at the front of his shirt. My father's fists, the way everyone called me Hill Deveraux's whore hurt, but not like he could, because I didn't love them. "Hill," I whispered as my vision blurred.

"I have no photos of you looking at me, Sarah. Trust me, I've looked over the past few months. Not. One. Why?"

A tear slid down my cheek as I rubbed the soft fabric between my fingers. His camera was magic; it revealed truths. Oh, what he could have done to me if he had seen what the pictures would show him.

"Even now when I took your picture. Now, when I've seen what haunts you, what makes you strong. You still fucking hide from me." He didn't shout the last words but I knew he wanted to. Hands cupped my face and he tilted my head back.

"I have these dreams where I'm standing in front of that fucking headstone only there's a date and it's almost four years old because I was too late. I wake up and I can't breathe, Sarah. I can't breathe and you're not beside me. I fear that maybe it wasn't a dream, that maybe you're dead and the actual dream was showing up on your porch. So I have to call my brother every night for reassurance. No matter what damn time it is he tells me you're okay, you're not dead, because I fear if I dial your number I'll get some recording saying this number is no longer in service."

I caressed his neck as he took a hard, deep breath.

"And I wonder," he said, his voice hoarse, "that if I had maybe seen even a glimpse of what you hide from me, that maybe you wouldn't have thought that was your only way out."

Hill. I wrapped my arms around his neck and pressed against him, holding him close. *Sorry, I'm sorry.* It was a startling realization to discover I had the power to hurt him too. When had that happened? "Stop, Hill. Stop," I whispered as I pressed my face into the curve at his shoulder.

"I can't do this anymore, Sarah," he mumbled into my neck. For a minute I thought he meant us and it made me panic. Like the knowledge he had this house to come home to. He eased my head back and took my mouth in a desperate kiss.

I met the greedy thrusts of his tongue with my own, afraid for myself. Since he'd come back two months ago, I had done everything I could to push him away. If I made him leave, he wouldn't come back again. I couldn't survive him walking away again.

"Shit. Damn it." He wrenched his head away and let out a string of creative curses.

"What?"

"According to Jax, this is what we do." He rubbed his thumbs over my cheeks as he stared down at me. "Our bandage is sex and it's why we're a fucked up couple. I see something that rips through the camera to my soul; I make it go away using you. You get hurt; you make it go away using me. And here we are again, avoiding the ouch with me wanting to get you out of your clothes and up into our bed."

Our bed? We had a bed? "William, look at me." He exhaled loudly but met my gaze. "I tried to hide my hurts in a bottle. Not you. Never you," I whispered and shut my eyes briefly to find the strength. I could do this. I could do this. Only *this* was more terrifying than taking him into my studio because that had been something that had happened to me. This *was* me. "Why me? Out of all the girls in Pierce Point, you kept coming back to my door. Why?"

He murmured my name. "I already told you that in your bathroom. Weren't you listening? You know me, Sarah. You know the selfish parts; you know the ugly parts. When Big Jack kicked me out what did I do?"

He had shown up at my door. Dazed. Lost. Angry. I understood what it was like to have a parent hate what you were. My father hated me because in birthing me, my mother had died. It hadn't been my fault but to Brandon James, she had been taken from him. His pain had morphed into anger then into hate. "But why?"

"You see me, Sarah. Me. Despite all my shit, you see me. I'm not William Hilton Deveraux to you. I'm not the son of Big Jack, even disinherited. I'm not a prize. God knows, I'm not a prize. When we went for pancakes that first morning, it wasn't me Sally saw. It was an extension of Big Jack. When your sister hit on me, it wasn't me she saw. It was a fat wallet because of my camera."

"She hit on you?" My eyes narrowed and Hill smiled.

"It's Brandi. I have a penis, and I wasn't broke anymore. Now shut up and stay with me here. My own father couldn't see me because of his pride. But you do. And because you always saw me, I was able to see me when things became too blurred in my head. You're my lens, Sarah. A little twist here, a little turn there, and suddenly I could see me again. I suddenly worked again. But through all my needing to see me, I forgot something."

I stared into those storm cloud eyes as I waited for him to go on. "Maybe I was too selfish, maybe I didn't even want to see beyond me," he said as he searched my face, "because there was this girl who was just as lost and blurred as me. More so. I'm bouncing it back to you, Sarah. No more lens caps, no more bullshit. Why do you let me back in after I'm an asshole to you? Why do you hide from me?"

"Because I love you," I admitted, unable to look away from his gaze this time.

He nodded as he lowered his head and gently kissed me. "Sarah mine," he whispered against my mouth. "Don't hide that from me. Okay?"

"Okay," I whispered back.

"It took a while to figure my shit out, but I did. I always came back to that crappy town because of you. I always came back to you. I will *always* come back to you. Know that, Sarah. Believe it. Believe me. I'd have come for you had Jax called me, because it's you. It was always you."

I nodded as he kissed me again, a slow but greedy kiss that made everything tingle. "We have a bed?"

He smiled and it was all bad boy Hill Deveraux. "Yes. Yes we do."

"I like my studio."

"You're gonna love our bed then."

I did.

SARAH

"Sarah."

I opened my eyes at the whisper of my name. There was a soft click then Hill lowered the camera. "Got you," he said with a wicked grin. He leaned down and kissed me. "Someone's at the door. Probably Jax come to give me shit for taking you to bed instead of to the barbecue." He tossed one of his shirts my way. I drew it on and liked wearing something of his. I sniffed it and felt all fluttery on the inside. The grin on his face followed by the wink added to that intoxicating feeling. Holy hell…happiness with Hill Deveraux. Who knew that would happen?

"He does like his lectures."

"Up and at 'em, sexy. You have Deverauxs to dine with and we don't like waiting." He left me in our bed. *Our* bed. I rolled over and pressed my face into the pillow that smelled of fabric softener. New sheets. According to Hill, he hadn't slept in the bed since he had bought it after he moved in. Too big and empty, he'd said, shadows of his nightmares in his eyes.

I heard Hill talking, a male voice responding, and I shut my eyes. I didn't want to go to a barbecue. As much as I adored Jax, I didn't want to go visit with him tonight. I wanted to stay here.

My skin began to feel itchy and the feeling of being watched pricked at me. Turning my head toward the source, I opened my eyes.

My heart stopped.

It stopped in my chest to see large dark eyes looking at me. Hair the same brown as mine was messed up and there was a streak of dirt on his cheek. His arms were on the bed, his hands stacked so his little chin rested on top. Automatically I reached down to tug the sheet up even though I was wearing Hill's shirt. I felt vulnerable all of a sudden in a way I'd never imagined. What should I say? Jesus.

I was going to kill Hill. Kill him. He had no right. No right!

I couldn't even remember the last time I had seen him. A baby. Small. Crying. Because his mother was a messed up failure. Something hot and painful twisted inside of me as I looked at Billy staring solemnly at me. I had given birth to him. He was beautiful. I had given him up because I hadn't wanted to ruin his life. Oh God, he was beautiful.

"Hi," he whispered.

"Hi." *Sorry, I'm sorry. I'm so sorry.* The words pounded in my brain and I swallowed over the knot in my throat.

He climbed up onto the bed and propped himself up on his elbows, pressing his face close to mine.

"Do you feel better now?"

I nodded.

"Daddy says you were really sick."

I nodded again. "Yes. But I feel much better."

He pressed a finger beneath my eye. "My mom," he whispered as if in awe then leaned forward and kissed where he had touched. "Did you miss me?"

I nodded, unable to talk because I would cry all over this little boy. I cleared my throat and brushed his hair off his forehead. "Every day, Billy. Every day." My hand was shaking. He lowered his head beside mine then wrapped an arm around my neck, hugging me tight.

It broke me apart. I had hurt him, betrayed him in ways he could never understand. And here he was, hugging me. I hugged him, the small, sturdy weight of a boy who had thrived without me, despite me. "I'm sorry," I whispered as I smoothed down the messy hair that was like his father's. He smelled of grass and sun, with faint traces of barbecue smoke. It made me look at the doorway where Hill leaned against the frame. "Thank you," I mouthed at him. He had done this. I knew it. This had Hill Deveraux written all over it. Sneaky Deverauxs.

He winked, lifted his camera and took our picture.

chapter thirteen

HILL

IT HAD BEEN a long time since I had seen Sarah scared, where that haunted girl slid through her eyes. I wasn't happy to see her return. Quietly she slipped into the room and stood there, staring at the man idly shuffling through my pictures. I wanted to punch him in the head, then throw him over the back deck where the water could have his body. It wasn't entirely logical, this possessive jealousy, but it was there.

This guy had intimate knowledge of Sarah.

It wasn't that I knew I was the only man who ever had sex with her, but I was going to be the last. And this one…he had left his mark.

Donovan Riley. Nice guy, I guessed. When he had knocked on the door, he had given me a look. Guess my reputation preceded me. His hair was messed up either on purpose or nerves because the kid's hair was the same way, only brown like Sarah's instead of bleached out bone white like his dad's. The kid looked like his dad. But for his hair and eyes. I'd know those big brown eyes anywhere. They even had the same hint of sadness to them. Wasn't that just a bitch.

He has a name, asshole.

The name made me uncomfortable. Billy. Billy who was eying his camera like he wanted to drag it home with him. Bound and determined to not be a fuckhead, I beckoned Billy over. Curious, he looked from me to the camera to his dad, then back to the camera. "You look through there and if everything looks nice and pretty, you press this button here." I pointed the camera at Sarah who still stood unnoticed by this Donovan guy. She was looking at him like she had looked at me that first day – like he was her worst nightmare.

It was nice to see someone else get that look. She rested her head against the corner of the wall and watched as the kid looked through the viewfinder, his attention pretty serious. It made me grin and a tiny smile appeared on Sarah's lips. "Now," I whispered. Billy seemed to agree because he caught that smile and those brown eyes watching me.

Two. Two pictures of her looking at me. Not too shabby.

"Hello, Donnie."

Donovan looked up and exhaled so heavily he puffed

his cheeks out. "Sarah." He stood, wiped his hands on his jeans, then dropped my pictures on the table. Reaching over, I tidied them up. Both my namesake and I watched the interaction with an intensity. "You look really good, Sarah."

Fucker. She looked beautiful.

"Thanks." Her gaze shifted to me and I wanted to hustle the Rileys out of my home, because she looked so uncertain, so ashamed of her past. She had lived. She had conquered all those demons in her head. She had no need to be ashamed. The ones who should be ashamed were Donovan and me. We had let her slip and slide down into the shit, happily going on with our lives and leaving destruction and heartache behind us.

Yeah, I very much wanted to throw the guy's dead corpse off the back deck.

"What are you doing here?"

She gave me a glare and I grinned, fiddling with my camera. Feisty Sarah was much better than sad Sarah. Feisty Sarah was going to get dragged back to bed if she kept that up. Slumping in my chair, I aimed the camera not at her but at Billy, who was leaning on the coffee table, staring at the photos of Sarah. The yearning in the boy's eyes was heartbreaking. I focused on the curve of his cheek, the little nose and the thick lashes. I was seeing less of his father and more of his mother. He leaned down until his nose almost touched a close-up of her face and I caught the image.

"I heard you were in an art show."

This time she blatantly looked at me and I shook my head. I would never tell someone that she was putting her demons out there for the world to see. They were personal and tragic. I had hurt her enough in the past.

Donovan reached into the back pocket of his jeans and handed her a folded piece of paper. She flattened it out and stared at it. Probably a flyer.

"But what are you doing…*here?* I told you." Her voice faded away as she looked at Billy. My chest felt like she had reached in and dragged my heart, kicking and screaming, out through the ribs. Billy looked up as if he knew where that sentence was going. Mother and son wore the same look. Sad, lost, broken.

"Hey, Billy," I said, setting the camera down. "Do you like to paint?" Sarah's eyes looked at me from the face of a child. Fuck. He was killing me. "I have got the coolest set up downstairs."

As we passed the couple facing off, I squeezed Sarah's hand. "Hey. Nothing you will regret, okay?" At her nod, I hustled Billy downstairs to set him up on one of the easels. "Did you know your mom draws?"

Yeah. I did it. I dropped the M-word.

"She does?"

"And she's really good. But I bet you're better. You look like you got some mad skills with the paint brush. Let's see if I can figure this out and you come pick out the colors." I lifted him onto the custom built cupboards and looked at a world that was beyond my understanding.

Camera and film. Simple. Easy. Not really knowing what Sarah preferred, I may have gone a little overboard, but it had been comforting to come down here and see these pieces of her world. Even if she hadn't been here.

Fuck, I had missed her.

"Your mom was really sick for awhile, Billy," I said as I held up a tube of blue paint. He shook his head and pointed at a lighter shade. "For a really long time, she was also really sad."

"Why?"

"Some people were really mean to her." *Some.* Understatement of the century.

"This boy at school, he's mean. He pushed me and I scraped my elbow." He lifted his arm to show the long gone wound. "He got a time out and I got a Spiderman Band-aid."

"Sweet. It made her really sad when people were mean to her, because they didn't get a time out. Nobody. So they just kept being mean." They. Me. Fuck. "And she kept getting sadder and then she got sick. It took her a long time to get better."

"Is she going to die?"

I thought of the headstone Jax had bought her, of that drawing. Jesus. She could've died. I was never going to be okay with that. Never. "No." Not just no but hell no.

Billy nodded once, as if because I had said it, Sarah would be okay. "I'm going to paint her a picture so she's never sad again."

"You know what? That's a great idea. I think I'm going to do one for her too."

Billy grinned and gave him a thumbs up. Always good, I decided, to get the approval of your girl's four year old.

SARAH

I couldn't look at him and I didn't know how Donnie could look at me. How he could, after all these years, keep trying to get in touch with me. Folding my arms over my chest, I walked through the room and stepped out onto the deck. He followed. Of course he did.

"Hill Deveraux, Sarah? Really?"

Flinching, I ignored Donnie and went down the stairs to the second level. His feet stomped heavily as he followed. Of course he did. "I'm sure he's 'Donnie Riley, Sarah? Really?' Don't be a douche." I rested my elbows on the railing and looked down at the view. I could hear the laughter of little girls and the scent of barbecue sauce, meat and charcoal drifted down. "You don't know him, so don't…do this."

"I know you named our kid after your fuck buddy."

"If you're here to fight with me, you can go home. I did the best I could at the worst possible time. I'm sorry that I'm this horrible human being but you weren't exactly perfect either." He was a nice guy but his attitude had been *a vagina in every bar.* Mine just happened to be the one in Pierce Point he decided to play in. He had been no more ready for a kid with a one night stand than I had been.

He could say what he wanted about Hill Deveraux, but at least he came back. Donnie couldn't exactly say the same thing. "You have no right to judge, Donnie. No right."

He rested his forearms on the railing a foot or so from me, his attention on the descent to the water. Jax had done an amazing job with this house. I wanted to explore until I found all the pieces of beauty he had put into it. "I know. This art show…tell me about it."

I didn't want to, because he would want to see it. And I didn't want him to see the table drawing. "No."

"Sarah, come on. I'm not even being a dick."

A grin appeared on his face and it reminded me of

why I had fallen into bed with him. He could be charming when he wasn't being a, well, dick. I told him, because I was proud of the show. I wasn't looking forward to it, though. Not in the least. It was me at my worst. It was me at rock bottom. It was me dying. And while putting the images to paper had been cathartic, all that was still inside of me.

I looked over my shoulder, rubbing my chin along the sleeve of my shirt. Through the windows I could see Hill and Billy at two easels. That perfect little boy had come from me. And that not-so-perfect man loved me.

"I'm sorry I was a bad mother." I watched Billy, a paintbrush in his hand and the end covered in blue paint. There was an intense look of concentration on his face and it stunned me that he was here.

"Like you said, you were doing the best you could at the worst time." He turned, watching that little human being we had made. Two strangers forever joined because of one little boy. "But, Sarah, that was then and this is now. He wants to know you. He's always asking about you and my knowledge is slim. It's not like I can say I banged you after a show then knocked you up. So I told him we'll make a list of all the things he wants to know about you. It's a long list. He wants to know what your favorite food is, what you want from Santa, do you have a dog, when can he come see you, maybe you'd want to go to the aquarium with him or go watch whales, or even just go to the park with him. He's four and he just really wants to know his mom. He wants her to read stories to him. He wants her to kiss his knee when he falls."

I looked away, my chest growing tighter with every wish he told me. "Stop."

"He loves me. I know. And that will never change but god damn, Sarah, look at him. Look! You don't have to be scared of him. You really don't. My mom thinks I'm insane for doing this. I guess she has visions that you're cracked up and hooking or something. But you're not. You're clean. You're sober. You look…you look…" Donnie exhaled as he met my gaze. "You were the walking dead when I met you. It didn't really matter to me because you had a willing vagina. And I know exactly what that makes me. So we'll see how the day goes. He's not that scary, Sarah."

I looked at Donnie, then I looked at Billy. My heart was ready to leap out of my body. I wasn't ready for this. Didn't he know I was a mess and couldn't be trusted around his son? Billy looked out the window and saw we were watching. He beamed at me, waved his hand that held a paint brush covered in blue then returned to his art.

Oh man.

I rubbed my hand over my heart. How could this

possibly end well?

SARAH

There was a person sleeping on me. Soft puffs of warm exhales tickled me as Billy slept. He smelled of grass, little boy, and wood smoke from the fire pit the Deveraux brothers had lit up a while ago. Jax's little ones had been put to bed long ago while Matt's still seemed to have some pep in them. They had shown Billy all their favorite toys, including the treehouse Matt had built. He had been a little shy, realizing he was with a whole bunch of strangers. Donnie watched and talked to the brothers. He was a reassuring presence for Billy, but mostly he kept to the background. Letting us stumble through this.

I still thought Donnie was insane for doing this. Who did this? Seriously? For all the man knew, I was a still a hot mess who shouldn't be trusted with a child.

Just watching him had stressed me out. What if he got hurt? What if he got scared? Who was I? I was nobody. A stranger. And yet here we were.

And now he slept. On me.

About an hour ago he had come over, climbed onto my lap and hadn't moved. He had sat with me, listening to the Deverauxs while twisting a strand of my hair around his finger.

And now he slept.

There was something to be said about a sweaty boy snuggling into me. My fingers brushed over his hair, smoothing down the wild strands. It was starting to hit me.

I had made this little person.

Somehow, some way, he had survived having me as his mother. A couple of survivors were we. A warm hand slid along the back of my neck and I tilted my head back to see Hill leaning on the back of my chair. His damn camera was aimed down at us and when I stuck out my tongue, he took the picture.

"You ready to go home? These guys can go all night, but you have an early morning. And Donnie should get this little guy into bed."

My arms tightened automatically. Nodding, I con-templating the physics required to get out of the chair while holding a child. "Good night," I told everyone.

"Good night, Sarah mine," Jax said as he grinned.

Hill grunted, then put his hand on my back, walking me to Donnie's car, the other man following. "Well, we didn't kill each other. Go us."

"Miracles are amazing."

He pinched my ass and I chuckled. Donnie opened the back door and showed me how to strap him into his car seat. He didn't even stir. Bracing my hands on my thighs, I gazed at this boy. *My* boy. Holy shit. Holy shit.

"You did good, Sarah," Donnie said with a grin. "And nothing went wrong. I'll call you in a few days. And this time…we're talking."

He climbed into the driver's seat and we stood there, watching the taillights disappear. My arms felt surprisingly light and empty. I wished I could remember him as a baby. He had been small, and that alone had terrified me. I should remember more than the fear.

Hill took my hand and walked me into the room where his photos were in boxes. Was this the living room or family room? It was hard to tell.

I decided to call it the furnished room because it was. When he sank onto the couch, he tugged me down.

"Not too shabby, Sarah mine. Not too shabby at all."

I rested my head in the little hollow between his shoulder and pecs. We both smelled of wood smoke and charcoal. "I'm scared about tomorrow," I admitted.

"More scared than when Donovan showed up with your kid for the first time in four years?"

I started to nod, shook my head then nodded. Both were pretty equal on the fear scale.

"And yet look at how well you did. Stellar name by the way." He draped his arm over my shoulders and played with my fingers.

Blushing, I avoided looking at him. "You haven't

asked me why."

"I'm a smart guy. I figured it out."

I arched my back so I could look at him. He gave me a sad but soft smile. Maybe he had figured out that I had really wanted Billy to be Hill's. But between the surgery and everything else, that wasn't in the cards. A moment of fantasy. I slipped my fingers between his and admired the different size. "If I asked, would you not come tomorrow?"

"No." He curled his fingers around mine. "I've already seen the drawings, Sarah. Do they scare me? Yeah, I can't lie. Do they hurt? Absolutely. Do I wish I had the ability to travel through time and change just one moment in those drawings? Fuck yeah. But here's the thing, we've seen the worst each other has, right?"

Nodding, I listened to the solid beats of his heart.

"And if I have to watch others see our past, then I will because you are. Then when the show is over, we're both letting it go," he whispered. "I don't want to see that headstone in my head anymore, Sarah. I don't want to think that one little thing could've changed the outcome of your overdose. I don't want you to look at me and see all the times I failed you. We'll have bad moments, because we're not living in la-la-land, but we can stop doing this. I need to stop doing this with you. So fuck yes, I'm coming tomorrow."

"Good," I nodded, pulling his arm close. "Good. Because I don't think I can do it alone."

"You're not alone. Never again. Got it?"

I nodded. "You too," I said quietly. His fingers tightened on mine and he pressed his face into my neck. He pulled me onto his lap and his embrace was hard as if he needed to give the hug. "Wherever you go, whatever you see, you're not alone because I'll be right here waiting for you to come home."

I wrapped my arm around his neck. "Sarah mine," he breathed out, making me smile. We just might make this work.

epilogue

HILL

ONE YEAR LATER

SOMEONE WAS ON my back deck, their bare feet braced on the middle railing. Sun shone over the entire deck, welcoming me home after a way too long trip that had ended with way too long delays. Fourteen hours to be exact, and my temper was shot. My back pack felt like it weighed at least one hundred pounds. I smelled like vomit thanks to the bad flyer beside me who had drunk a lot of vodka, and all I wanted was my bed and a shower. If I could manage both at the same time, that would be perfect. I knew those feet. Only one person would be on my back deck at this hour. I fisted my hand over the strap of my bag as I saw the drawing pad balanced on thighs, a cup of hot chocolate on the arm of the chair and a leg draped over hers.

I didn't know it was a weekend, but then again I was

pretty happy to know I lived in B.C. Pretty much every weekend Billy was with us and watching him and Sarah bond had been amazing. He sat on her lap, watching her draw. I loved watching her do what she loved. Her art show had been a nightmare because of all that art, not just hers. Glimpses into people's soul was hard. Her overdose drawing had sold, and Jax, the dick, had hung it up in my dark room as a reminder. Him and his god damn lessons.

I'd take seeing anyone from my family at this point because the month away had been long and draining.

Anyone.

But I was so glad it was her. Because my heart was doing stupid, crazy things like beating a little faster in anticipation of seeing her. Sarah mine. My lover, my best friend, my wife and thanks to a corrective surgery, soon to be mother of my kid. Shit. I was going to be a dad. Who the hell thought that was a good idea?

She looked over and she smiled slowly at seeing me. She lifted Billy off her lap, scrambled out of the chair and came at me.

Why me? Out of everyone in Pierce Point, why had she picked me?

Because I was a pretty lucky bastard.

William Hilton Deveraux was home.

acknowledgments

This book wouldn't be without some serious back up and support. There's my awesome beta-readers Sloane Taylor, my good friend Patricia and Steena Holmes, who believes in this story as much as I do. There's my amazing editing team of (again) Patricia, Bobbi Beatty and Alyssa Palmer. Kate Laurens who generously gave me some real estate in her Safe Haven novella. And those who kept pushing me to hurry up and get this book out: Steena Holmes and Tawny Stokes. Thank you, ladies, for being my bra with this book.

Want more for your naughty To Be Read pile?

Check out Jenna's other books:

Scorpio Stings

Scoring Lacey

Sarah Mine

With Vivi Anna

The Vampire Affair Part Three

The Vampire Affair Part Four

And on the deliciously naughty BDSM side

Domme for Cowboy

Yield

Erotica

Her Surrender

bio

Jenna's writing dreams truly began one summer on the air mattress of her childhood home. There she tackled her first romance: a truly wretched attempt at a medieval historical. Upon finishing the purple prose laden story of (in her own words) crap, Jenna decided that perhaps the historical genre wasn't for her and she promptly began to write in a contemporary setting. If only the journey had been easy. She tackled category romances (and in her own words) felt like they were crap. She didn't have the patience for romantic suspense. Really, she just wanted to get to writing the sex. (hint hint, Jenna) Her romantic comedies were so traumatic that she stopped writing until one day she got a phone call from a friend who said "We can totally write this." The genre was erotic romance and it was (in her own words) like coming home. Residing in Calgary, Alberta, Jenna happily writes the naughty romances that make her mother sooooo comfortable. (not)

www.jennahoward.com